GABRIELLE TOZER

Melody
Trumpet

📚 Angus&Robertson
An imprint of HarperCollins*Children's*Books

Angus & Robertson
An imprint of HarperCollins*Children'sBooks*, Australia

First published in Australia in 2019
by HarperCollins*Publishers* Australia Pty Limited
ABN 36 009 913 517
harpercollins.com.au

HarperCollins*Publishers*
Level 13, 201 Elizabeth Street, Sydney NSW 2000, Australia
Unit D1, 63 Apollo Drive, Rosedale, Auckland 0632, New Zealand
A 53, Sector 57, Noida, UP, India
1 London Bridge Street, London SE1 9GF, United Kingdom
2 Bloor Street East, 20th floor, Toronto, Ontario M4W 1A8, Canada
195 Broadway, New York NY 10007, USA

A catalogue record for this book is available
from the National Library of Australia

ISBN 978 1 4607 5497 9 (paperback)
ISBN 978 1 4607 0936 8 (ebook)

Cover illustration and design by Risa Rodil
Typeset in ITC Stone Serif by Kelli Lonergan
Printed and bound in Australia by McPherson's Printing Group
The papers used by HarperCollins in the manufacture of this book are a
natural, recyclable product made from wood grown in sustainable plantation
forests. The fibre source and manufacturing processes meet recognised
international environmental standards, and carry certification.

For Sienna,
who makes everything extraordinary

1.

The Trumpet heir is born

Melody Trumpet burst into the world with a screech that rattled the windowpanes of Trumpet Manor. It was a perfectly ordinary sound for a newborn baby startled by the cold air, yet the doctor and nurses gasped at the shrill wail. The world expected the daughter of opera superstar Viola Trumpet and renowned conductor Barry T Trumpet to have a voice so beautiful that even the hardest, coldest person would cry tears of joy at a single note.

Years of the Trumpets winning awards and touring the globe with orchestras, ballet companies and theatre troupes had set the stage for this moment. The long-awaited appearance of this cherub was supposed to be *extraordinary*. That was what everyone expected, from the doctors and nurses, to the international press waiting outside the manor for news of her arrival.

The expectation had been set thirty-nine years earlier, when baby Viola's first teary gurgles were so sweet and harmonious that the nurses had swaddled her in a soft woolly wrap and carried her from cot to cot to calm the other newborns with her song. And now Mrs Viola Trumpet was the face of opera around the world — an icon whose voice box was insured for millions of dollars. As far as the Trumpets were concerned, it was perfectly acceptable for ordinary babies to shriek out of key. But not a Trumpet. Especially not one deemed a medical marvel!

Mrs Trumpet had been told by doctors for years that she could never have a child. She'd almost given up hope until one day the impossible became possible and she was granted her wish.

A daughter.

An heir.

A gift from the musical gods.

Mr Trumpet had fallen to his knees and sobbed with happiness at news of the miracle, his moustache drooping low as it filled with fat tears. For nine months, he conducted the air around Mrs Trumpet's belly morning after morning, night after night. Music from his thirteen award-winning classical compositions soared around the nursery, bouncing off the lemon and peach walls that had been decorated with musical notes.

The Trumpets were considered music royalty across the globe. Year after year the duo received so many awards and honours that they needed to build a new wing in Trumpet Manor to house them. Mrs Trumpet had received more curtain calls than anyone in history, twelve distinguished authors had written books about her and Mr Trumpet's brilliant careers, and they had so much money they didn't know what to do with it all.

They were certain their wondrous miracle child would carry on the musical legacy of the Trumpet name. In preparation, they placed their unborn baby on the waiting list for the Battyville Elite School For Musically Gifted Children — the most prestigious and selective music school in the world. Mr and Mrs Trumpet had met there as children, and now giant oil paintings of them adorned the school's many hallways and staircases for the more *ordinary* students to admire and dream of maybe one day being half as talented. The Trumpets dreamed of the day their child would become the rising star of the school, then of Battyville, then the country, then the world — just as they had done.

But dreams don't always come true — as it was discovered when baby Melody squawked her first out-of-tune note and then wailed into the wee hours.

'Honeypot, what shall we do?' Mrs Trumpet asked her husband, rocking a red-cheeked Melody in the pair's enormous four-poster bed. 'The beastly creature won't shut up.'

'My darling Viola, there must have been a mistake,' Mr Trumpet assured her. 'A Trumpet would never make such a terrible noise. That doctor owes us an explanation. Somehow they've misplaced our little angel.'

'Oh, that horrific bleating sound! We'll be a joke,' Mrs Trumpet hissed. 'Laughed out of the town! All our plans, our dreams ... and our reputations. Barry, our reputations!'

Mr Trumpet scooped the screaming baby into his sausage-like arms and stroked her mop of straight jet-black hair. 'We'll work it out. With a little guidance she'll find her way.'

Mrs Trumpet began to sob. 'She's no bigger than a watermelon but she sounds like a snoring rhinoceros! Or a freight train! Or a rhinoceros snoring on a freight train!'

Mr Trumpet stared down into Melody's big chocolate-brown eyes. They were the same colour as his own. 'We're Trumpets, Viola. We'll set things right — whatever it takes.'

She nodded. 'You need to fix this, Barry. No one else can ever find out that our baby is not at all extraordinary.'

'Yes, my darling.' Mr Trumpet squeezed her hand. 'Consider it done.'

4

But what could he do?

Despite growing public interest, the Trumpets hadn't yet dared to hold a press conference or send out a media release announcing Melody's arrival. Too much was at risk. Their entire musical legacy could be obliterated with just one of Melody's squeals.

Melody. Even her name, which meant 'a sequence of single notes that is musically satisfying', was now almost too painful to utter aloud. Melody hadn't been born with the voice of an angel like her mother. In fact, she seemed about as musical as a gumboot.

What would people say if they discovered the Trumpets' prodigy was just a crying, pooping baby like any other?

Mr Trumpet did the only thing he could think of in such dire circumstances: he and his wife starved the world of all information about their heir. Everyone assumed she was a child prodigy who remained in seclusion to focus on her training, and naturally the Trumpets didn't correct the assumption. In fact, they fuelled it by refusing to answer any questions at all about Melody. Any journalist who asked even a single question about her was banned from interviewing the Trumpets ever again.

To maintain the secret, Melody spent much of her childhood in her wing of Trumpet Manor. A high-security fence ran all around the grounds so no one could spot her on the rare occasions when she was allowed outside. She was home-schooled by a private academic tutor, and friendships were banned the way other parents banned sweets. Forget about joining a dance class or sports team. Banned. Forget about using a mobile phone or spending an afternoon in the library or at the park. Absolutely, definitely BANNED.

Aside from the Trumpets' driver and bodyguard, Royce, and their housekeeper, Miss Sprinkles, the only other person privy to the family's secret was a man by the name of Mr Pizzicato. He was one of the greatest music teachers the world had ever known, and the Trumpets paid him an outrageous amount of money to become Melody's music tutor when she turned three. He was to give her private instrument and vocal lessons in a secret soundproofed room inside the Battyville Elite School For Musically Gifted Children.

Mr Pizzicato's greatest achievement to date was tutoring a chicken named Clive to become one of the most beautiful-sounding soprano opera singers to ever grace the stage.

'Mr Pizzicato will find Melody's talent and make her a true Trumpet,' Mr Trumpet declared as he and Mrs Trumpet waited for Mr Pizzicato to walk down the steps of the private jet they had sent for him.

'Remember your performance with Clive in Venice, my darling?'

Mrs Trumpet nodded. 'Oh yes. And Melody will be better than that feathery diva once Mr Pizzicato is done with her. She'll be the best!'

And so Melody's private music lessons began. No one, not even Principal Sharp, ever saw her enter or leave the school. Royce drove her in the family limousine to a secret entrance every morning at eight thirty on the dot, where Mr Pizzicato met her and ushered her through a twisting, turning secret corridor high above the classrooms to the private studio that had been built with money donated by Mr and Mrs Trumpet. The routine was performed in reverse at the end of each day when it was time for Melody to be escorted back to Trumpet Manor.

Over the years, Mr Pizzicato and Melody clocked up thousands of hours of lessons. Singing, musical scales, theory, improvisation, and every instrument you could think of. Thousands of hours — with no improvement. Not even a little.

And with every day that passed, with every dollar spent, Melody grew more and more aware that she was the thing her parents despised more than anything else. She was completely, utterly and painfully *ordinary*.

2.

An unhappy birthday

Ten candles burned on Melody's seven-tier, rainbow-coloured ice-cream cake. Taking centre stage was an extravagant cake-topper — a small and edible version of Melody in a sparkly purple dress singing into a microphone. Miss Sprinkles had outdone herself with the birthday cake this year.

She clapped her hands, then leaned over to straighten the red headband and green bow in Melody's long jet-black hair. 'Well, blow out the candles!' Miss Sprinkles said in her usual excitable and breathy voice. 'And don't forget to make a wish, my sweet Melody. Turning ten is a special day, you know. What are you waiting for?'

Melody glanced at her mother's empty seat at the head of the long, narrow dining table. She'd rushed off to take an urgent phone call five minutes into dinner and hadn't returned. She'd already missed the entree and main course. Melody didn't want her to miss dessert too.

Her father was sipping his drink and rewatching an old clip of himself accepting a Hall of Fame Award. He spent most dinnertimes reminiscing about the golden years of his career as a conductor. Even on Melody's birthday.

'Mr Trumpet, sir, Melody's cake is ... well, it's ready,' Miss Sprinkles said. She pursed her lips and pointed at the ice-cream cake, which was melting into a lopsided mess.

'My word!' Mr Trumpet broke away from the clip to see the cake and its fiery glow of candles looming towards Melody. 'Quick, blow them out, child!'

'I'll wait,' Melody said, steadying the leaning tower of cake with her spoon. 'We should enjoy it together, as a family.'

But her father was absorbed in the screen again.

Shaking her head with disappointment, Miss Sprinkles took her place behind Melody, who hadn't shifted her gaze from the cake. The big grandfather clock ticked away the minutes, accompanied by an occasional sigh from Miss Sprinkles or a satisfied grunt from Mr Trumpet as he watched the old footage.

By the time Mrs Trumpet burst through the doors, red feather boa flying, Melody's birthday cake was a sugary puddle that had oozed over the edges of the plate and soaked into the tablecloth. The candles, all fizzled out long ago, were now just black streaks through the technicoloured ice-cream.

'We have a problem,' Mrs Trumpet announced to Mr Trumpet. She didn't seem to notice that her daughter was sitting in front of the destroyed cake with her head hung low.

Mr Trumpet sat up, startled, knocking his cutlery onto the floor. 'What is it, my fuzzy coconut?'

'You're not going to like this one bit. It's that's nosy principal from the school!' Mrs Trumpet stopped and glared at Miss Sprinkles, who was taking her time picking up the dropped cutlery.

Miss Sprinkles lowered her head and said, 'I think I'm needed in the kitchen. Happy birthday again, my sweet Melody.' And she scuttled off, a stack of plates rattling in her arms.

Melody licked melted ice-cream off her fingertips, not saying a word.

Mrs Trumpet took a long gulp from her glass. 'Do *you* know what year it is, honey crumpet?' she moaned to Mr Trumpet. 'It's *the* year!' She paused, realising Melody was still in the room. 'Ah, child, you can go to your wing now.'

'But Mother, it's my birth—'

'To your wing!' Mrs Trumpet repeated. 'I have something important to discuss with your father.'

Melody bit her lip. It was clear where her mother's priorities lay. She swiped her finger through the melted ice-cream again and stood up to leave.

'Where are your manners?' Mrs Trumpet scolded with a raised eyebrow. 'This is not a household for wild animals.'

'Thank you,' Melody whispered as she pushed her chair in under the dining table, then did a quick curtsy.

Mrs Trumpet's eyes remained cold as she released a thin-lipped smile. 'Good night, my child. Sleep well.'

Melody nodded, mumbled, 'Thank you, Mother,' and left the dining room.

As the door clicked shut behind her, a wild-eyed Mrs Trumpet turned to her husband. 'Oh, sugar plum, it's happening — all our worst fears. Principal Sharp has just delivered the most terrible news, and for once there's nothing we can do!' She dabbed at her heaving bosom with a lacy white handkerchief. 'She has personally invited the entire family, including Melody, to a *very* public event.'

'Send her another generous contribution,' Mr Trumpet said, returning his attention to the screen, where he was now receiving an award for his fourth concerto. 'That should keep her off our backs for another year.'

'Barry!' Mrs Trumpet said, swatting him over the head with her handkerchief. 'She called to personally invite us to see Melody's first performance in Crescendo Hall.'

'What?' Mr Trumpet spluttered. 'Why on earth would Principal Sharp be excited about that? Melody's awful!'

'But she doesn't know that, you buffoon!'

'Oh yes.' He sank back into his seat. 'Of course she doesn't. But why does she think Melody's going to be performing in Crescendo Hall of all places?'

'Because she's inviting us to the annual Debut Gala,' Mrs Trumpet said. 'Apparently, the child is ten years old.'

'Ten years old, you say? You're joking!' Mr Trumpet snorted in disbelief. 'When did this happen?'

'I checked her birth certificate as soon as I got off the phone. She turned ten *today*. How did we let this sneak up on us?' she moaned.

The Debut Gala was the most important annual event at the Battyville Elite School For Musically Gifted Children. As soon as a student reached ten years of age, they gave their first performance in the school's great Crescendo Hall, which was one of the most famous concert halls in the world — in part due to the famous performances the Trumpets themselves had given there. Melody's tenth birthday was a day the Trumpets had been dreading ever since her first ear-piercing cry as a baby.

'What on earth shall we do?' Mr Trumpet pondered, rubbing his enormous belly. 'I tell you what, call that snooty-nosed Principal Sharp and tell her what we've always told her: Melody Trumpet is a genius who needs to be left alone to practise. Any interference will only disrupt her prodigious progress.'

'That won't cut it any more, pumpkin,' Mrs Trumpet hissed. 'Melody is ten! She has to perform at the Debut Gala or she'll be ... Ohhh, I can't even say it!'

'Publicly exposed!' Mr Trumpet moaned. 'We'll be the laughing stock of the solar system.'

'It gets worse. That nosy principal wants to arrange a private rehearsal this week to gauge Melody's progress. *This week.*'

'We'll work this out,' reassured Mr Trumpet. 'Tell Principal Sharp that Melody can't meet with her this week because she has a ghastly cold. She can't get out of bed, let alone sing.'

'A cold?' Mrs Trumpet scoffed. 'What are we — amateurs?'

'Alright, maybe she's ... broken a leg,' Mr Trumpet suggested. 'Or she's busy recording her first album.' He snapped his fingers with glee. 'Or perhaps she's on her way to perform for the Prime Minister.'

'The Prime Minister is overseas at the moment.'

'Wait, I've got it! I've ripping got it!'

Mrs Trumpet huffed. 'Well?'

'Melody can't make it because she's doing the first ever performance on the moon,' he cheered. 'Yes, that's it! She's in an exclusive zero-gravity environment learning how to perform in space. Sharp can forget meeting up with her this week ... because Melody is booked out until the Gala!'

Mrs Trumpet contemplated the idea for a second, then rolled her eyes. 'Zero-gravity? Performing on the moon? You've lost it. Unless ...' She paused again. 'No, you've definitely lost it. We're done for!'

'Take a breath, my little honeydew,' said Mr Trumpet, sipping on his drink. 'I'll call Principal Sharp and thank her for the lovely request, but decline because the Trumpet heir's calendar is already bursting at the seams with appointments and obligations booked months in advance. We simply cannot change her schedule at this late stage. After all, it takes dedication and focus to be a prodigy.'

'Especially a fake one,' Mrs Trumpet said.

'Oh, my darling, I know it won't ward off Sharp forever, but —'

'But it will buy us more time. I know. Thank you, my cuddly caramel tart. I knew I could count on you.'

'Whatever it takes, remember?'

Mrs Trumpet sucked in a breath. 'Whatever it takes. And after you've spoken to Principal Sharp, call Mr Pizzicato and remind him what's *really* on the line here. He and the child have a lot of work to do — for all our sakes.'

3.

The special invitation

'I've never seen one this fancy,' the postman told Melody through the gap in the gate as he passed the envelope to her. It was silver with gold foil edges that glinted in the sunlight. 'It's not someone's birthday, is it?'

Melody shook her head. Her tenth birthday had come and gone months ago, with just a melted rainbow ice-cream cake to mark the occasion.

The postman chuckled. 'By the looks of that embossed gold, you'd better get your finest frock ready. Expecting an invitation for high tea with the Queen, are you?'

Melody wasn't. She never expected an invitation to anything. But she smiled her most polite smile at the postman, then hurried back to her corner of the garden as soon as he'd gone.

She looked over one shoulder, then the other. Her parents were nowhere to be seen. On the other side of the lawn, the groundskeeper, Mr Bloom, was crouched in the dirt and whispering to his beloved roses. Melody listened to him happily whistle and hum as he tickled their petals and watered the soil around them. He sounded as out of tune as she did in Mr Pizzicato's private tutoring sessions.

Behind Mr Bloom, his three wild-haired children lazed on the grass under an old tree, watching a group of ducklings marching towards a small pond. Today they were barefoot, and, as always, they were laughing. The eldest, a boy around Melody's age, stood up, plopped his baseball cap on his little sister's head, then launched into a wobbly cartwheel. His siblings' eyes widened with delight and they clapped.

It wasn't the first time Melody had seen Mr Bloom's children playing in the grounds of Trumpet Manor. She'd overheard Miss Sprinkles telling Royce in the kitchen one night that Mr Bloom was a widower, which was why the children spent many afternoons by his side or playing in the manor's famous garden maze. Melody often saw them while she was curled up in the shade, scribbling poems and daydreams into her brown leather-bound notebook. But, like everyone else in the world, the Bloom children were forbidden to talk to her, and she was forbidden to talk to them. So they stayed on their side of the garden, and she stayed on hers, with nothing but her notebook to keep her company.

The notebook had been a present from her parents on her ninth birthday. Like most years, they'd forgotten to organise a suitable gift or celebration, so Mr Trumpet had grabbed the nearest item from a cupboard in his study and wrapped it up in old newspaper and ribbon. Yet that time their forgetfulness had paid off. The notebook was the perfect gift for Melody, and it had barely left her side for over a year.

Now, with the postman gone, and the Bloom family distracted, Melody glanced around one last time to make sure there was no sign of her parents. Sure that she was alone, she held up the envelope. Her name danced across it in neat loopy calligraphy: *Miss Melody Trumpet.* This sort of thing didn't happen every day. In fact, this sort of thing *never* happened.

She turned the envelope over in her hand. It was from *Ms A F Sharp of the Battyville Elite School For Musically Gifted Children.*

Allegra F Sharp. The school principal.

Heart racing, Melody slid her finger under the sticky seal of the envelope, edging it open millimetre by millimetre. She didn't dare move too fast in case it ripped.

Inside was a folded piece of silver paper with gold foil edges to match the envelope. With a few gentle tugs, Melody slipped out her first piece of mail.

The Battyville Elite School For Musically Gifted
Children's Annual Debut Gala

Dear Miss Trumpet,
It is with the greatest pleasure that we request your presence at our upcoming Debut Gala in Crescendo Hall.

We would be delighted if you would make your debut at the Battyville Elite School For Musically Gifted Children on the first evening of spring by performing a solo piece of your choosing. Not only would you headline the Debut Gala, but the event will be a celebration of your family's enormous successes.

The Prince and Princess of Zanjia will also be in attendance as our special guests to witness you, the heir of the extraordinary Viola and Barry T Trumpet, take your rightful place on stage.

The evening is sure to be a highlight for the school and our entire community.

I look forward to hearing from you soon.

Your principal,
Allegra F Sharp

Melody reread the letter in a rush, then folded the paper in half and slid it back into the envelope. What a lovely invitation. Her first. But she knew she wasn't ready for a public performance, even though Mr Pizzicato had been working for years towards this very moment.

The Trumpets had often spoken of the school's prestigious Debut Galas over the years — tales of extravagant gowns, standing ovations, international guests and show-stopping performances, often their own.

Her mind ran over the details of the invitation:

A solo piece of your choosing.

Headline the Debut Gala.

The Prince and Princess of Zanjia.

The heir of the extraordinary Viola and Barry T Trumpet.

The first evening of spring.

That was just a month away!

Melody gulped. Maybe the invitation wasn't as lovely as she'd first thought.

* * *

Melody pressed her nose against her bedroom window, watching her parents sashay towards their limousine in the driveway. Mrs Trumpet flirted and laughed with Mr Trumpet, twirling her feather boa around, before Royce ushered her into the back seat of the limousine.

The Trumpets were off to their weekly croquet session at their country club, which meant they'd be gone for the rest of the afternoon.

Melody nibbled on her thumbnail and turned her attention to the pale blue baby grand piano in the corner of her bedroom. It had been a fourth birthday present from the school board. *A sign of things to come*, the card had read. Mr Trumpet had ripped it up and none of them had ever spoken of it again.

Her gaze moved to the hot pink electric guitar and purple saxophone leaning against her bookshelf. She had hours to practise if she wanted to. But she didn't want to. The instruments looked so perfect, and Melody already knew she couldn't play them — not the way a real Trumpet would.

She plopped onto her bed, reached under her pillow and pulled out the envelope. She peeled it back to reveal the invitation, and traced her fingertips over its gold embossed edges, cringing as she remembered how Principal Sharp had invited her to *take her rightful place on stage*. She was going to be exposed as a huge fraud.

Her imagination ran wild with the headlines that would blast around the globe:

HORRENDOUS TRUMPET HEIR!

TRUMPET'S A FAKE!

OUT-OF-TUNE TRUMPET!

Her parents would appear on the television news, wiping away tears as they apologised to the good people of Battyville. Meanwhile, Melody's heart would feel heavier still, because she'd let down the people she wanted to make proud: her parents and Mr Pizzicato.

But what if I don't let everyone down? she thought. *What if I surprise everyone for a change?*

How would she prepare for the Debut Gala? Where should she begin?

Melody thought of her mother twirling her feather boa as she walked towards the limousine ... then it hit her! She knew just where to start.

After slipping the invitation back under her pillow, Melody tiptoed out of her bedroom and into the hallway. She hurried down the sweeping staircase to the grand foyer, slipping in her polka-dot socks on the freshly polished floor, then up the other sweeping staircase that led to her parents' wing.

As she approached the top step, loud humming echoed from the dining room. Melody froze, then peeked in to see Miss Sprinkles crouched beneath the table, wearing fluffy white headphones as she hummed and scrubbed the floorboards. Holding her breath, Melody continued past her and into her parents' bedroom.

She paused at her mother's dressing table to size up her reflection in the enormous gold-plated mirror.

Her fingers traced over the pewter dishes filled with trinkets and jewels, and the collection of peculiarly shaped perfume bottles — and paused on a small burgundy bottle with dimpled edges and a thick tassel. It had been a gift from her father on the night her mother was honoured with her third Most Outstanding Performer Award. Melody remembered the evening well. She'd been sent to her own wing for the night, as usual, but had snuck out to sit on the top step of the staircase to watch her parents leave for the party in her mother's honour. 'I spray just a smidge, my handsome poppyseed,' Melody remembered her mother telling her father. 'Just enough to leave people wanting more.'

Melody held the perfume bottle above her, just like she'd seen her mother do, and spritzed the air with two hard bursts. Her nose wrinkled as the smell of roses filled the room. Spluttering, she walked through the scented mist.

On her mother's bedside table stood a black-and-white photo of a younger Viola Trumpet on stage at the International Music Awards, her arms filled with trophies. Mr Trumpet was in the background, beaming with pride and holding a number of trophies of his own. The photo wasn't colour, but Melody knew the trophies were gold. For the Trumpets, the trophies were always gold.

She entered her mother's walk-in wardrobe — the silliest of names for a room that was twice the size of Melody's bedroom. The walls were adorned with shelves covered with trophies and treasures. Brightly coloured gowns, skirts, blouses and coats burst from hangers in every direction. Melody plucked a hat with an enormous peacock feather from one of the many hatstands and plopped it on her head. Next, a pale yellow feather boa, which was so long she snaked it around her neck three times and it still dragged along the carpet.

She skipped past a rack of dresses, and paused in front of another jewellery box. She lifted the lid and peered at the diamond bracelets and gem-laden necklaces inside. She selected a rose-gold cuff and slipped it onto her arm. It was so big it went all the way up to her shoulder. Swallowing, Melody reached into the box for a pearl ring that she knew was her mother's lucky ring. She'd recorded every chart-topping album while wearing it.

The ring slid off Melody's pointer finger, so she put it loosely on her thumb, then stood in front of a full-length mirror with gold trimming. She faked a high-pitched laugh, like her mother's whenever they had company.

'Why, yes, I am *the* Melody Trumpet,' she said to her reflection, putting on a posh voice to rival her mother's. 'Yes, daughter of Viola and Barry T Trumpet and heir to the Trumpet throne.' She curtsied. 'I am delighted to be here at the annual Debut Gala, Principal Sharp, what an honour.' Melody paused, eyebrow raised, feigning embarrassment as she clutched her hand to her collarbone. 'A genius, you say? Little old me? That's very kind of you, but I simply can't accept. Well, if you insist ... oh, you do insist?'

Melody waltzed over to her mother's shoe collection: an assortment of rainbow-coloured, leopard-print and patent-leather heels, boots and sandals. Without removing her socks, she pressed her feet into a pair of cream strappy heels.

'If the shoe fits ... Oh, please don't mention that genius word again, Principal Sharp!' Melody waved the feather boa at her reflection. 'Are the rumours true? I can't say much ... I can't, I shouldn't ... but yes, okay, all the rumours are true. My talents are *extraordinary*. There is nothing ordinary about me. Nothing at all.'

She spun in the heels. 'Melody by name, Melody by nature! I'm off to the Debut Gala and everything will be — ooomph!'

Melody tripped on the rug and fell backwards into a stand dripping with rainbow scarves. As it crashed down, she became tangled in metres of long, flowing fabric and knocked over a pair of silver heels, which sent her mother's entire shoe collection tumbling like dominoes around the room.

'Oh no,' Melody said, looking around at the mess. 'No, no, no, no, no!'

The door creaked open and a worried face peered through the crack. 'Hello in there,' Miss Sprinkles said, her voice shaking. 'You should know I'm moments away from calling the police!'

'Wait!' Melody cried.

'The manor will be surrounded in seconds. Our Battyville boys in blue don't waste any time.'

'Miss Sprinkles, hold on! It's me!'

'Melody?' Miss Sprinkles burst through the door, clutching a pile of fresh towels with the Trumpets' personalised monogram to her chest. 'My goodness,' she stammered, taking in the sight of Melody surrounded by mountains of clothes. 'Your mother will skin you alive for touching her things! Do you have any idea what all this is worth, what trouble you've got yourself into? We have to clean this up at once.'

'I know.' Melody took off the feather boa and hung it back on the nearest stand. 'I didn't mean to make a mess.'

Tears welled in the corners of her eyes. It had felt so wonderful to be *someone* for a few minutes, even if it was only make-believe. A genius — adored, appreciated and glamorous, and fit to perform at Principal Sharp's annual Debut Gala.

Miss Sprinkles crouched down. 'We'll tidy this all up and pretend it never happened. But you must never come in here again, sweet Melody. You have no idea how it feels to disappoint your mother. She has certain ... expectations.'

Melody wiped her eyes and didn't say what she was thinking.

She knew how it felt to disappoint her mother.

She knew better than anyone.

4.

Hoping for a miracle

Tension filled the room as the Trumpets and Mr Pizzicato sat around a cheese platter in the manor's dining room. Mr Pizzicato gnawed on his fingernails, which were already chewed down to the quick. Mrs Trumpet sloshed her drink onto the floor with every frustrated gesture, while Mr Trumpet slathered a thick slab of blue-vein cheese onto a cracker and shoved it into his mouth.

The silver envelope with gold foil edges, now covered in crumbs and wine stains, lay next to the platter. Melody had given the invitation to her parents upon their return from the country club and they'd immediately called an emergency meeting with Mr Pizzicato.

'An audience ... the spotlight on her ... the Prince and Princess of Zanjia! It's not possible,' Mr Pizzicato whispered, running his hands through his thinning grey hair. 'I've tried everything with Melody, ma'am, *everything* ... and all for nothing. Seven years of my life sacrificed for this family.' He groaned. 'How did we think this day would never come?'

'We need you to fix this, Pizzicato,' Mrs Trumpet said. 'We're almost out of time.'

Mr Pizzicato cleared his throat. 'I fear it's not possible. I've spent decades working with the best. But I can't crack *her*. If word gets out that I've failed to conjure musical talent from a Trumpet of all people ... well, I'm doomed. My career will be over. You have to tell Principal Sharp that Melody can't do the Debut Gala.'

'Not an option,' Mr Trumpet said through a mouthful of cheese. 'She's ten. It has to happen. Imagine if a Trumpet was exposed as a fraud ... there *is* such a thing as bad publicity, Pizzicato.'

'I'm at a loss,' Mr Pizzicato said. 'The trombone, the alto horn and the cornet are out. And you don't want to know what happened with the trumpet, or the tuba or the French horn.'

'What about the helicon?' Mrs Trumpet asked, topping up their goblets. 'The mellophone? The flugelhorn?'

Mr Pizzicato dry-retched, and took a second to recompose himself. 'My ears are still ringing after

Melody attempted the flugelhorn. I should mention that the bassoon and oboe are also *most definitely* out.'

'What about the string instruments?' Mr Trumpet said, cracker crumbs flying from his mouth. 'The woodwinds? The bagpipes? She must take to *something*.'

'The brass sounded ghastly, and the strings literally snapped at her touch,' Mr Pizzicato said. 'As for the bagpipes, it took several days for my hearing to return.'

Mrs Trumpet clutched her heaving chest. 'This is a nightmare!'

'Even the violin?' Mr Trumpet asked. 'We've always been fond of the violin.'

'She broke eleven violin strings last week alone.' Mr Pizzicato hung his head. 'I've never seen anything like it.'

'Are we certain she can't sing?' Mrs Trumpet asked. 'With her gene pool, I just can't understand it!'

'Please, ma'am, I can't bear another minute of listening to Melody attempt to follow in your footsteps. It's not going to happen.'

'But you got that blasted chicken to sing!' Mr Trumpet said. 'You're telling us you can't do the same with our daughter?'

'And need we remind you that your teaching services came highly recommended all those years ago,' Mrs Trumpet said, stepping closer to Mr Pizzicato and baring her lipstick-covered teeth. 'It's the *only* reason we hired you.'

'My reputation is unparalleled, but I'm not a magician,' Mr Pizzicato said, wringing his hands. 'There is no one in the world who could get a single note out of Melody that's worth listening to. I'm sorry but it's true!'

Mr Trumpet slammed his fist on the table. 'What are you trying to tell us?'

'The same thing I've been telling you for years,' Mr Pizzicato said, arms flailing. 'She's a delightful child and my affection for her is great, but Melody doesn't have a musical bone in her body. In fact …' He paused to take a huge gulp from his goblet. 'I believe it's time for me to hand in my resignation. Perhaps you will find a magician to replace me who is able to conjure talent from an empty well.'

The Trumpets swapped dark looks, their lips cemented into stiff lines. They knew they'd never find such a person. Mr Pizzicato was the best music tutor in the world.

'We want you to finish the job we paid you for,' Mrs Trumpet said. 'You're a music teacher, so teach her music! We saw the footage of you training that baboon to play the piano.'

'And let's not forget the chicken,' added Mr Trumpet. He got up to massage Mrs Trumpet's shoulders with his enormous zucchini-sized fingers. 'I saw him on a commercial the other day. You made him a star.'

Mr Pizzicato took another gulp. 'With all due respect, Clive the Chicken has more musical talent in his beak than Melody has in her entire body.' He sucked in a sharp breath. 'My deepest apologies ... but Melody is no ordinary child.'

'Actually, she's *entirely* ordinary, Mr Pizzicato, that's the problem,' Mrs Trumpet said. 'We do not accept your resignation. You have a month until Melody is headlining the Debut Gala, and she *will* be ready. We're not asking if you can do this. We're *telling* you to do it. Do you understand?'

Mr Pizzicato held up his hands in defeat. 'I can't perform miracles.'

'All our reputations are on the line here.' Mrs Trumpet sighed. 'We'll cancel her other academic studies until the Debut Gala is over so she can fully invest in this. And if it's money you're worried about, that is no object. Buy every instrument in Battyville, in the country, if you have to. Hypnotise her, make her practise around the clock — hire a real sorcerer to help for all I care. Just get it done.'

'Ma'am, I —'

Mr Trumpet cut him off. 'Pizzicato, you are our only hope. I know you care about the child, so if you won't do it for me and Viola, do it for her. Don't you want to see her achieve something after all this time?'

'It is all I've craved for many years.'

'Excellent,' Mr Trumpet said. 'Then you will do it.'

Mr Pizzicato nodded. 'I will try my best.'

'No,' Mrs Trumpet chimed in, 'you will *do* your best.'

'Discretion remains essential, you hear?' Mr Trumpet added.

'It has always been a secret, and it will remain one until Melody is ready,' Mr Pizzicato said. 'You have my word.'

Mrs Trumpet raised her glass and clinked it with Mr Pizzicato's. 'And ready she shall be. We look forward to seeing Melody's star shining on stage at the Debut Gala.'

5.

Claudette Rouge and the Debut Gala gown

While Mr Pizzicato focused on getting Melody performance-ready, Mrs Trumpet threw herself into a different priority: what Melody would wear to the Debut Gala. More specifically, what gown made by Claudette Rouge, the most sought-after designer in the country, Melody would wear to the Debut Gala. It was all Mrs Trumpet could talk about, and today was no different.

'We're almost there,' she squealed, clapping her hands together as Claudette Rouge's sandstone-brick building appeared through the limousine window. 'Can you see it, child? Can you?'

Melody looked up from scribbling the beginning of a new poem in her notebook and gave a small nod as their limousine came to a stop.

'Now don't drag your feet,' Mrs Trumpet whispered with an excited giggle as she and Melody slipped out of the limousine. Royce tipped his hat at Mrs Trumpet from the front seat. 'Hurry, Melody, we can't be late when Claudette has closed the studio just for us. And sunglasses on — we don't want the paparazzi hounding us. Well … not today.'

'Yes, Mother,' said Melody, sliding her notebook into her pocket and struggling to keep up with her mother's brisk pace.

'Smoke and mirrors may be all we have,' said Mrs Trumpet, lips pursed. 'You will need a *spectacular* dress to accompany your *spectacular* performance at the Debut Gala. And I will need a gown too.'

Spectacular performance. Melody gulped. She knew her parents were disappointed in her progress so far. She'd caught Mrs Trumpet weeping into her fluffiest feather boa the previous night.

'So I really have to perform?' she asked her mother now. 'Mr Pizzicato seemed worried at practice yesterday. Well, more worried than usual.' She recalled the vein in his forehead that had looked ready to burst through his skin.

'There's no choice,' Mrs Trumpet said, striding along. 'We're out of options. And we're putting all our resources into this, so it's time for you to step up and play your part. It's that or … we'll have to send you to boarding school somewhere far away, where no one knows the Trumpet name or heritage. I'm not sure where that would be — your father and I are adored globally after all — but surely there must be *somewhere*.'

'Please don't send me away,' Melody said, her voice cracking. 'I'm trying, I promise. And I'll keep trying. I'm just no good yet.'

'You're the Trumpet heir. You're not supposed to be good — you're supposed to be *great*.' Mrs Trumpet's hand grabbed Melody's and squeezed it tight. But it didn't feel like a reassuring squeeze. It felt anxious. 'You have the Trumpet blood after all,' Mrs Trumpet finished.

'The finest blood,' Melody parroted. She'd heard her father say it endless times.

'Mr Pizzicato insisted I return you to school within the hour to continue your practice,' Mrs Trumpet said, shooting Melody a look. 'What are you working on today?'

'The drums.'

Mrs Trumpet shuddered. 'Thank goodness we soundproofed that studio. He's running out of time, you know. Make sure you tell him that, child.'

'Yes, Mother.'

Mrs Trumpet released Melody's hand to touch up

her lipstick. 'Now, we mustn't dilly-dally. These gowns will be on every best-dressed list for the next year.'

Claudette greeted them at the door with a fire-engine-red smile and so many air kisses that Melody lost count. A measuring tape swung from around her weathered neck.

'Viola, you look marvellous as always. How have you been, you dazzling creature?' Claudette squawked, not waiting for an answer as she thrust a flute of fizzy pink champagne into Mrs Trumpet's manicured hand. She gaped down at Melody. 'Why hello, sweetie. I've been waiting for this day. How fabulous that you'll be making your debut at the Gala in one of my designs.'

'*So* fabulous!' Mrs Trumpet beamed and gave Melody a small nudge as they entered the store. The walls were pale pink and gold chandeliers hung from the ceiling. 'Isn't this fabulous, child?'

'Mmm-hmm.' Melody forced a smile for Claudette as she soaked in the scent of vanilla candles burning in the store. She wished she could pretend things were fine too. But Melody was tired of pretending — especially when she showed zero signs of improvement during music practice.

'Let's begin!' Claudette announced. She positioned Melody on a pink poof in front of a rack of glitzy gowns then shuffled behind the counter to retrieve an oversized sketchbook. Mrs Trumpet purred with approval as Claudette flashed pages and pages of dress design sketches in front of Melody, never waiting to hear her opinion on any of them. There were stunning jewels, intricate beading, delicate lace — each gown was more lavish than the last. 'On your feet, sweetie!' Claudette continued, as she prodded and poked Melody, spinning her around and sizing her up with her measuring tape.

Claudette paused to nibble on her fingernail. She stared at Melody. She muttered to herself. She furrowed her brow.

'I've got it!' she cheered, clapping her hands together with such force that Mrs Trumpet almost dropped her drink. 'A sweetheart neckline, beaded crystals on the bodice, tulle flared skirt with an inbuilt petticoat for maximum volume ... and let's do it in a rich emerald to make Melody's eye colour pop. It will be a gown fit for music royalty.'

'Perfect, Claudette,' Mrs Trumpet said, raising her glass. 'But will such a magnificent gown be ready in time for the Gala?'

'I'll see to it personally,' Claudette said with a flamboyant flick of the wrist.

Melody hid a wry smile. At least *something* would be ready for the Debut Gala.

'And for me?' Mrs Trumpet hinted, batting her thick eyelashes as she sashayed around the store. Her gaze landed on the rack of gowns behind Melody. 'The child can't be the only Trumpet stealing attention at the Debut Gala.'

'Viola, you couldn't hide from the spotlight, no matter how hard you tried.' Claudette beamed. Melody tried to imagine a world where her mother tried to hide from the spotlight. Impossible. 'These couture gowns have all been designed with you as my muse — so please, take your pick,' added Claudette. 'My team and I have been working on them day and night. Would you like to try one on?'

Mrs Trumpet sipped her drink. 'One, two ... or all of them!' she announced, striding into the nearest dressing room. Claudette heaved the first gown – a jet-black mermaid cut – from the rack and hurried after Mrs Trumpet, measuring tape flapping behind her.

Melody plopped down on the poof with a sigh. So much for rushing through the appointment to get Melody back to Mr Pizzicato. This was going to take all day! While her mother fussed and preened in the dressing room, Melody pulled out her notebook. Her eyes skimmed one of her poems, tracing over the letters.

Just once,
Just once I'd like to be,
In the kind of place that's in my head,
The perfect place for me.

She smiled at the rhythm of the words, feeling them almost leap off the page.

Where it's all okay,
And it's all alright,
And nothing is a pain.
Where the sun's not too hot,
The clouds aren't too grey,
And no one hates the rain.

It was one of the first things she'd ever written, right after her parents gave her the notebook. She flicked through the pages, reading other words from her past. Mrs Trumpet was still busy trying on gown after gown with Claudette — not that Melody was bothered. Time disappeared when she got lost within her notebook.

Waiting and hoping,
For someone to see,
The girl in the tower,
And what she could be.

But life just goes on,
And things stay the same,
So from a distance she watches,
Away from the game.

Yet one day she's certain,
That someone will see,
The girl in the tower,
And what she will be.

Melody smiled at the words.

'Enough of that!' a shrill voice scolded above her, and the notebook was suddenly snatched from her hands. 'Didn't you hear what I said?' Mrs Trumpet stood over Melody, her face screwed up into a taut angry mask, the notebook raised high above her head. 'I asked you to thank Claudette for the great honour of designing your Debut Gala gown, but instead you sit here with your nose in some silly *book*?'

'I ... I didn't hear you,' stammered Melody.

'No, you weren't listening,' Mrs Trumpet hissed, as Claudette hurried to hang the couture dresses back on their hangers. Forget one spectacular gown for Mrs Trumpet – she was buying the whole rack. 'We are doing everything in our power to make you a star and *this* is what you're paying attention to?'

'It's just a notebook.'

'I'm not investing all my time, money and energy into you for this tripe! Do you not understand the pressure this family is under? I'm getting rid of this rubbish. Right now!' Mrs Trumpet stuffed the notebook into her handbag.

'Mother, please!' Melody pleaded.

'We're leaving,' Mrs Trumpet added, gulping down the rest of her drink. 'I'm so sorry, Claudette, I'm mortified and can't handle a moment more.' Mrs Trumpet spun on her heel away from Melody and teetered over to Claudette's side. 'Kisses, darling!' she gushed, kissing the air between them. 'You've been a dream, as always. I'll send Royce for the gowns soon.'

Mrs Trumpet grabbed Melody's hand and strode out the door onto the street, blowing Claudette a final kiss over her shoulder. Melody expected to walk back to the limousine but instead Mrs Trumpet veered towards a nearby rubbish bin, heels click-clacking on the cement, and dropped the notebook into it. Melody rushed to retrieve it, but Mrs Trumpet stuck out her arm and blocked her from reaching into the bin.

'It's time you focused on what matters to this family: *music*. The Debut Gala is less than a month away for goodness sake! Other children would kill to be in your designer shoes, not to mention enjoy a private fitting with Claudette Rouge. And this is how you repay me? No gratitude at all.'

'You can't do that,' Melody said, her face reddening as she strained against her mother's outstretched arm. 'That notebook is mine.'

'I am Viola Trumpet and I can do what I please. It's time you started acting like a Trumpet too, even if you have to fake it at first.'

Melody's jaw tightened. 'Well, maybe I don't want to be a Trumpet if it means being more like *you*.'

Mrs Trumpet's eyes narrowed into thin black slits as she wrapped her long fingers around Melody's arm and yanked her away from the bin.

'No, please! My notebook!' Melody screamed as Mrs Trumpet dragged her back towards the limousine.

Twisting in her mother's grip, Melody looked over her shoulder and saw a tall man in a suit dump a half-eaten container of pasta into the bin, coating her notebook in thick red sauce.

'No! Stop!' she cried. 'My notebook!'

But it was too late.

Her writing. Her thoughts. Her heart. All gone.

6.

Mr Pizzicato's last shot

The doorbell of Trumpet Manor rang, playing the opening bars of Mr Trumpet's Triple Concerto Number 3 in E Minor.

'Here we go,' Mr Pizzicato said to Melody, his hand hovering over the doorknob.

Melody drew in a deep breath. She wasn't ready, and she knew Mr Pizzicato wasn't either, but they seemed to have run out of options for her Debut Gala performance. The most obvious solution — regular practice — hadn't worked. Lip-syncing had also been a disaster: Melody couldn't move her lips in time with the music, plus she was terrified of being caught out. Mr Pizzicato had tried auto-tuning her voice in his studio, but it had just sounded like a chipmunk was singing.

Melody's emerald gown from Claudette Rouge's had arrived, and still she and Mr Pizzicato hadn't come up with a better idea. Everything had come down to this moment.

The doorbell rang again, setting off the concerto.

'Should I answer it?' Melody asked. 'Or would that be strange?'

'Ah ...' Mr Pizzicato's voice trailed off. The situation was strange no matter who answered the door. 'It was my idea. I'll do it.'

He opened the door to reveal the most peculiar sight: a line of at least one hundred Melody Trumpet lookalikes winding their way from the front step down the staircase and along the driveway. Melody gasped. She'd never seen so many girls with red headbands and green bows pinning back their long jet-black hair. Her hand raced to the bow in her own hair. It was like looking in a mirror. An extremely bizarre mirror, where everything was the same only different.

She wasn't the only one staring at the line of lookalikes. Mr Bloom and his three children watched from a corner of the garden, whispering and pointing at the girls. His eldest son caught Melody's eye and gave her a friendly smile. She broke away, unsure how to respond — especially in front of a long line of chattering, laughing and singing Melodys.

Mr Pizzicato's face had turned an ashy grey. 'Unbelievable,' he stammered, before straightening his posture. 'One moment, girls. Be with you soon.' He closed the door and turned to Melody, his eyes wide and worried. 'Remember the back story?'

'You mean the lie?'

He sighed. 'We don't have time to go over it again. Do you remember?'

'Of course. We're holding auditions to find an understudy for a Melody Trumpet movie.'

'Exactly.'

'Except there is no Melody Trumpet movie. It's just the Debut Gala, and you're hoping to trick the winner into performing as me. And trick everyone else into thinking it *is* me.'

'Melody! Never say those words out loud again.' Mr Pizzicato pressed his finger against her lips. 'We can't give up now.'

'Or we could just tell people the truth?' She shrugged. 'I'm hopeless. There. Simple.'

Mr Pizzicato swallowed, then opened the door to call out, 'Nearly ready, girls. Keep practising your vocal warm-ups.' He slammed it shut again and crouched down to her level. 'Melody, do you know what I saw on the drive over here today?'

'No, Mr P.'

'First, the statue of your parents in Town Square, next to the ice-cream parlour. Then I saw a busker playing your father's first concerto. And lastly, as I arrived, an old woman pushing a shopping trolley of fruit and vegetables stopped me outside the gate and asked, "Sir, are you really going inside?" I told her, "Yes, today I am," and she shrieked with joy, as if I'd just said I was about to meet the Prime Minister. This isn't a joke. Your parents' stars may have faded a little, but they're still icons. We can't take this away from them. Or from the people. Because *they* will care.'

'But I'm just me,' Melody said.

Mr Pizzicato sighed. 'You're too young to know what you are, or what you could be.'

Melody rolled her eyes. 'Well, *you* don't know everything. Yes, you've taught a chicken to sing and a baboon to play piano, but do you know how to make a rocket fly to the moon?'

'No.'

'Or how to write a haiku?'

'Melody —'

'Or how to fold a fitted sheet like Miss Sprinkles can? Do you know why some people are poor and some people are rich? And why brussels sprouts and peas taste disgusting but are good for you, while lollies taste like happiness and are terrible for you?'

Mr Pizzicato sighed again. 'You know my field of expertise isn't lollies or brussels sprouts. But I'm begging you, Melody — we need to pull this off, because if we don't ... Well, frankly I don't know what will become of either of us.'

She noticed the slight quiver in his voice and nodded. 'Fine.'

'Miracles can happen, and we're certainly going to need one,' he said, fiddling with his bow tie. 'How does that look?'

Melody stood on her tippy-toes and straightened it. 'Perfect, Mr P.'

He ruffled her hair with affection, then straightened her headband and bow. 'Remember, you are the elusive Melody Trumpet. Let's keep it that way. You are a muse for these girls. A genius. But most of all, a mystery.'

'That's me,' she said, shooting him a wry smile. 'Alright, let's do this.'

Melody opened the door. The girl at the front of the line — a beaming blonde holding a jet-black wig — squealed.

'It's her!' she shrieked, thrusting a glittery red marker and a poster of a young Viola Trumpet into Melody's hands. 'Can I get your autograph?'

Mr Pizzicato shook his head. 'There will be no

autographs! This is an audition, and it starts now, so have a little decorum, please, everyone.'

'Sorry,' Melody whispered to the girl. She wasn't used to this sort of attention.

'She spoke to me,' the girl squealed, covering her mouth. She spun around to the other girls and shouted, 'Melody Trumpet spoke to me!'

Everyone buzzed with excitement.

'Quiet!' bellowed Mr Pizzicato. 'Anyone else who so much as whispers to Miss Trumpet will be escorted out by security. Now, please follow me. We haven't got all day.'

The girls filed up the steps and into the manor, clinging to each other with nerves and excitement. Their eyes widened as they took in the grand foyer and the two sweeping staircases leading up to the separate wings.

One girl murmured, 'This is just how I dreamed it would be. I've got to tell my parents. I've got to tell everyone everything … *Everything*.'

Mr Pizzicato shot Royce a look. Royce scooped the girl up in his arms, threw her over his shoulder and carried her out the door.

She began to cry and promised that she wouldn't tell anyone anything. 'Not a soul,' she sobbed. 'Not even my mum.'

Another girl couldn't resist inspecting a bowl of lemons displayed on a coffee table. 'Melody's probably touched these,' she whispered to her friend as she slipped a lemon into her backpack. 'It'll be worth a fortune.'

Mr Pizzicato gave the nod to Royce, who retrieved the lemon and carried the girl outside.

Mr Pizzicato climbed onto a chair to address the group of Melodys now crammed into the grand foyer. 'Is anyone else here other than to audition for the role of Melody Trumpet?'

The room fell quiet, except for a loud crunching sound. Everyone looked around for the culprit. It was Miss Sprinkles, gnawing on a carrot as she stared in awe at the Melody lookalikes. Her face flushed a deep crimson and she returned to wiping down one of the archways that led off the grand foyer.

'Come along then,' announced Mr Pizzicato, rubbing his lower back as he got down from the chair. 'To the theatre we go!'

The girls, many of them biting their lips to mask their excitement and stifle their 'Ooohs' and 'Ahhhs', followed Mr Pizzicato and Melody along the winding hallways of Trumpet Manor, past marble pillars and doorways and room after room, towards the theatre. Previously, it had only been used for Mr or Mrs Trumpet's birthday celebrations, and private concerts for VIP guests.

Melody plonked herself down in the third row of the plush red velvet seats, while Mr Pizzicato fussed about on stage with the other Melodys, handing out numbered tags and getting them into order. Then he ushered them backstage, and rushed out through the stage lights and down the steps to join Melody.

'There's more than one hundred people here to audition,' he said. 'I've got a good feeling about this, Melody. It might just work.'

Melody leaned forward, her elbows on the seat in front of her, her chin resting in her palms. It was time to see if any of these girls could be everything she wasn't herself.

7.

The auditions

'Melody One, you're up!' Mr Pizzicato bellowed into the darkness.

A spotlight sparked up on stage. A tiny girl, much shorter than Melody, toddled out from the wings and positioned herself in the yellow circle. Her hair was a fiery red, close to the colour of the seats, and her face was sprinkled with freckles. She pulled on a jet-black wig and squinted into the bright stage lights.

'You may begin,' Mr Pizzicato said.

After a small nod, she launched into a wobbly version of 'Humpty Dumpty'. Melody cringed. Did she sound this awful? Melody One's performance had only just begun, but the real Melody already wanted a pair of earplugs.

'Not great,' she whispered to Mr Pizzicato. 'Although

I guess that means she's nailing the impersonation of me.'

He swallowed a laugh, then pursed his lips. 'This is serious, Melody. Need I remind you again?'

Melody rolled her eyes, not that Mr Pizzicato could see her in the dark. 'Either way, she's not right. I'm sure she's positively lovely, but with those freckles, her height and voice, people will know immediately she's not me.'

'Thank you, that will be all,' Mr Pizzicato called out to Melody One, who was still stumbling over the lyrics. 'We appreciate you coming in. The exit is down the steps and to your left. Royce will escort you out of the manor.'

'Is that a no?' Melody One asked. 'Did I do something wrong?'

'I'm sorry, the voice isn't quite there. Keep practising and, ah, I'm sure there'll be other roles you'll be perfect for,' Mr Pizzicato fibbed, trying to soften the bad news.

Melody stared at her palms. She couldn't handle critiquing more girls like this.

But Melody One wasn't budging. 'Perhaps if Melody — hi, Melody! I love you! — could sing a line or two, I could do my best to imitate her?'

'We're very short on time,' Mr Pizzicato said. 'I asked for an extraordinary voice, and I'm sorry but you don't fit the requirements.'

Melody One nodded and hurried off the stage, wiping away tears.

'Was that necessary, Mr P?' Melody whispered. 'That was pretty mean.'

'The media will be more than mean to us if we don't nail the Debut Gala performance,' he said, his mouth cemented into a rigid line. 'It will be a bloodbath.'

One by one, each Melody filed out to perform, followed by a short, fiery whispering session between Mr Pizzicato and the real Melody.

'Melody Five is too pale.'

'Agreed. And too quiet.'

'Much too quiet.'

'I like Melody Twenty-Nine. She's got spunk. She's bubbly.'

'You're not bubbly.'

'I am too!'

'Melody Twenty-Nine is far too tall. If this was a normal production, I would cast her in a second. She's perfect in every other way. But she has to *be you* at the Debut Gala. We can't just slap a wig on her and hope that people don't notice the difference in height. There will be hundreds of people in the audience, and the media will be circling for any scrap of gossip. If they notice anything awry, we're doomed. Let's move on.'

'Fine. But I still like her. And I am bubbly.'

'Are not,' Mr Pizzicato muttered, before calling in the next Melody.

'Forty-Six is good.'

'Too squeaky.'

'What about Sixty-One?'

'Her voice is too deep.'

'Seventy-Two!' Mr Pizzicato called, then peered closer. A boy with strawberry blond hair beamed at Melody from the stage. 'What are you doing up there, young man?'

'Ah, hi, Melody,' the boy mumbled. 'Sorry to crash the auditions but I didn't know how else to reach you. Want to go to the movies with me?'

'Get out!' Mr Pizzicato shouted, as Melody slunk down in her seat in embarrassment. 'Seventy-Three!'

'Too beautiful — she looks like a movie star,' Melody said. 'My mother would love her though. Hey, maybe she could play me for the rest of my life, and I can go and relax on a tropical island? That way, everyone wins.'

Even Mr Pizzicato smiled at that.

By sunset, he and Melody had listened to one hundred and two girls audition, eaten three ice-cream sundaes with chocolate topping and cherries, and fallen asleep a total of thirteen times. Mr Pizzicato had to shake Melody awake when she began snoring through Melody Eighty-Eight's performance.

Just one girl to go.

Melody One Hundred and Three.

'This is it,' Melody said to Mr Pizzicato.

He sighed. 'If there was ever a time for a miracle ...'

The girl walked onto the stage. Melody sat up straight in her chair. The long jet-black hair was perfect. Her height was spot-on. Her mannerisms were similar, very similar — it wouldn't take long to perfect them.

'Hi,' Melody One Hundred and Three said with a smile.

Mr Pizzicato gasped. 'She's you! I don't believe it!'

'Are we sure I don't have a twin?'

Mr Pizzicato laughed, then paused as though he was contemplating the possibility. He shook his head. 'If only.' He waved to the girl. 'You may begin.'

She opened her mouth, but nothing came out. Her bottom lip trembled, and her eyes darted around the theatre before she burst into tears. Then Melody One Hundred and Three sprinted into the wings.

'Stage fright,' Mr Pizzicato muttered. 'That won't do at all.'

Melody One Hundred and Three's voice echoed through the theatre as she shrieked into her phone: 'No,

Mum! I can't! I won't! You can't make me!' A jet-black wig flew out from behind the curtains, slid across the stage and plopped into the front row of seats. 'I don't want to be an actor! I hate singing! You know that, Mum!'

Melody One Hundred and Three suddenly reappeared on the stage, tears streaking her cheeks. She ran down the steps, pushed the doors wide open and fled the theatre.

Mr Pizzicato sighed. 'Guess that's that then.' He flopped forward in his seat with his head buried in his hands.

Melody hurried down to the front row to retrieve the wig. It looked like a limp animal in her arms. She twirled it around her hand. 'What do we do now?'

'Nothing,' Mr Pizzicato said, snatching the wig from her. 'There's nothing more we can do. I'll see you at music practice tomorrow.'

Muttering to himself, he stormed past Melody, tossed the wig into a bin in the corner of the theatre, and left.

Melody sucked in a deep breath. She'd seen Mr Pizzicato defeated in the past, but never like this. Sighing, she walked up the steps onto the stage, staring down at the empty seats. The yellow glow of the spotlight warmed Melody's face as she imagined the theatre full of people munching popcorn and sipping drinks, applauding in all the right places, wiping away tears during the emotional moments.

She closed her eyes, feeling sick with nerves at the very thought.

8.

A sudden goodbye

Mr Pizzicato lay in silence on the couch in the secret soundproofed music studio inside the Battyville Elite School For Musically Gifted Children, his body frozen, his mouth slightly agape. It had been seven and a half minutes since he'd uttered a word to Melody.

'Mr P,' she said, putting down the glockenspiel mallet and waving her hand in front of his face. 'Are you alright? Shall I keep playing?'

Nothing.

Melody took a step towards him. 'Mr Pizzicato?'

Still nothing.

She returned to playing the glockenspiel, but froze when she heard a loud groan from Mr Pizzicato. Red with embarrassment, she put down the mallet and picked up a triangle and its metal beater. She hit the triangle and a rich, shimmering sound rang through the studio.

Mr Pizzicato sat up. 'Do that again.'

Melody readjusted her position, her palms and the backs of her knees suddenly sweaty. *Diiiiiiing*.

She looked at him.

'Again,' he repeated.

Diiiiiiing. Diiiiiiing. Diiiiiinnnnnnnnng.

'Stop,' he whispered. 'Stop, stop, *stop*. I can't believe it. It's … it's utterly *terrible*. I care for you like a daughter, Melody, but my ears can't take another second. I'm done. Defeated.'

Melody plopped down on the carpet. 'There's no cure for what I have, is there? This … *ordinariness*?' Her parents had used that word to describe her for years.

'No, Melody. It appears not.'

'And you can't teach me to be more like my parents, can you?'

'No, Melody. It appears not.'

Mr Pizzicato lay down again and pulled a blanket over his head.

'Mr P?' Melody said, rushing to his side. 'Should I call a doctor?'

A loud, drawn-out sigh came from beneath the blanket. His bushy grey eyebrows peeked out the top.

'No need. Just taking a second to plan how I'm going to fake my own death to escape this horrid mess. We may need a plan for you too.'

Melody couldn't tell if he was joking.

'I used to be good at teaching music. The best in the world, in fact. But for the first time, my techniques haven't worked. I remember the day your parents first brought you into this studio like it was yesterday. Your fuzzy little mop of black hair. Your pink rosebud lips. But that screeching. Oh, that screeching.'

Melody dared to peel back the blanket a little. 'Not everything can go to plan all the time, Mr P. I bet even the most brilliant people in the world thought they were failures after years of trying to split the atom, or land on the moon. And then one day they succeeded — because they never gave up. That's how quickly things can change. Mr Pizzicato … are you listening to me?'

No response.

'I know this isn't what you wanted for your life,' she continued, her voice a little softer. 'But maybe it's not what I wanted for mine either. And yes, we've been knocked down — many times — but we can try something different.'

We *have* to try something different, she thought, staring at the instruments all around the room.

'Different!' Mr Pizzicato threw back the blanket and sprang off the couch. 'You're right,' he said, punching the air. 'You're right, Melody.'

'I am?' Melody's eyes lit up. It may have been the first time he'd ever said those words to her. Maybe the first time *anyone* had ever said those words to her.

'I need a new plan,' he went on. 'I need to *try something different.*'

'Great! Want me to get some butcher's paper and textas? We can brainstorm —'

'No, Melody.' He walked to his desk and swept all his belongings into his briefcase.

'What are you doing, Mr P?'

'Trying something different.' He wriggled into his trenchcoat. 'I'm taking my first holiday ever — maybe on a tropical island somewhere, like you said the other day. That sounds marvellous. I'm buying a one-way ticket and I don't know when I'll be back. You should do the same. Enjoy yourself.'

'But ... the Gala. It's so soon!' Melody pointed at the calendar pinned to the wall behind his desk. Giant red crosses marked down the days to the event. 'What am I supposed to do? I have no one else to help me.'

'I'm sorry, Melody, I have nothing more to teach you. I am useless to you and your family, and I can't bear that feeling one second longer.'

'But when are you coming back?' Melody asked.

She waited for Mr Pizzicato to say it was all a mistake, that he wasn't leaving after all. That they would come up with a plan together for the Debut Gala. But he didn't.

He cleared his throat and ruffled her hair. 'I don't know. I don't know anything any more, it seems. It would be wise for you to tell your parents to hire a new music teacher. Yes, that would be best. And you may still use the studio to practise, of course. I won't be needing it anytime soon.' He passed her a shiny gold key. 'Here. Now, please close the door behind you when you leave, Melody.'

His voice cracked, and he quickly looked away to stuff some sheet music into his briefcase. But Melody was convinced she saw his eyes glistening.

'Goodbye, Mr P,' she whispered. 'I'm sorry.'

'No, Melody,' he said, looking at her again. 'I'm the one who's failed. I've failed myself, but worst of all for a teacher ... I've failed you.'

9.

Hello, Freddie Bloom

Fingers wrapped around her backpack straps, Melody stepped out of the secret passage that wound high above the classrooms and entered the school's main hallway. It was a last-minute decision, a small act of defiance. After all, Mr Pizzicato wasn't following the usual plan any more, so why should she?

Her heart raced with the fear of getting caught. Not that she should have worried: no one paid any attention to the tiny girl with the red headband and green bow in her hair. Her feet barely touched the ground as she was swept up in the stampeding mass of children racing outside for lunch. She struggled to breathe as she was squashed against lockers and stinky armpits.

Then, suddenly, everyone was gone, spilling out of the swinging doors at the end of the hallway. And

Melody realised she had no idea where she was supposed to go next, or what she was supposed to do. All the little lies had grown into a big, throbbing, *festering* lie that now seemed so huge it might explode.

She nibbled on her fingernail. Mr Pizzicato may have grumbled a lot, but he was the closest person to a friend she'd ever had. Now even he couldn't bear to be around her. She was all alone. Which meant she was going to have to work this problem out by herself.

Well, all alone except for a small boy with a baseball cap pulled down low over his scruffy brown curls who'd just charged out of the boys' bathroom holding a skateboard. His shirt was untucked, his too-short pants flapped at his ankles, and his jacket was faded and hung off his bony frame.

Their eyes locked. It was the boy with the wild hair. The eldest of Mr Bloom's kids.

It was clear from the way his eyes widened that he recognised Melody too.

'Hi,' he said, taking off his cap and revealing his messy mane.

'Hello.'

'I know you, don't I? You're Melody Trumpet.'

Melody blushed. It was rare to hear someone other than her parents, Royce, Miss Sprinkles or Mr Pizzicato say her name.

But then she remembered: it was against the rules to talk to other people. Not even the children of the Trumpets' staff. Her family's big festering lie loomed over her again.

'Um,' she stammered, 'I ... I have to go. Right now. You didn't see me. Okay?'

'Yes, I did. You're right here.' He beamed at her. 'Melody Trumpet mixing with us ordinary folk. I never thought I'd see the day.'

'No. No, listen.' Melody stepped closer to the boy. 'Please ... I wasn't here. My parents will kill me — or worse!'

He grinned another big toothy grin. 'What's worse than being killed?'

Melody fought back a smile. 'Just trust me. If you tell anyone, I'm done.'

'You mean grounded?'

Melody had essentially been grounded her entire life, but she nodded anyway. This was no time to explain the complexities of what was at stake. 'Something like that.'

'Righto. It's a secret then.'

'Thanks,' Melody said, turning towards the doors at the end of the hallway. She paused. 'I mean it. No one can know.'

'Who could I even tell?' he asked with a shrug.

'Principal Sharp, your father, my father … my mother.' She shuddered. 'You could tell everyone.'

'Well, I won't. Not even my goldfish, Bert. Not anyone.'

'Thank you, uh …?'

The boy crossed his arms over his chest. 'You don't know my name, do you?'

Melody went to protest, then shook her head.

'It's Freddie Bloom. But just Freddie is fine.'

'Okay. Well, bye, just Freddie.'

'See you round. In the garden … right?' He grinned at her again.

Melody tried again not to smile back. 'Right.'

'Here, take this.' Freddie passed his cap to her.

She looked at it in confusion.

'If you don't want anyone else to recognise you, you need this more than I do,' he explained.

'Okay, thanks.' Melody removed her headband and slipped on the cap. 'I'll find a way to repay you.'

He shrugged. 'It's just a hat. I'm good.'

She tried to think of something she could give him. 'Well, if you do need to tell someone you saw me, you can tell your goldfish. Secrets aren't always easy to keep to yourself.'

'Sounds like you're speaking from experience,' Freddie said. He laughed, then pretended to lock his lips and throw away the key. 'Nah, I won't tell anyone. Besides, that Bert is a real blabbermouth. Enjoy the hat, Melody Trumpet!'

* * *

Melody pulled down the baseball cap to disguise her face as she stepped over the cobblestoned strip that ran around the sides of Town Square. The air was thick with the sound of music, and rich with the smell of roast beef, sizzling onions and melted cheese radiating from the food trucks lining the street. It was the first time Melody had ever been there alone. She was enjoying being free to go at her own pace without Mrs Trumpet hissing at her to hurry up, or Royce encouraging her to get in the limousine before the paparazzi snapped another photo.

Melody stopped to pat an orange kitten that was scratching its claws on a wooden post. She ignored the statue of her parents looming large by the ice-cream parlour and stepped on the cracks in the pavers with abandon. This afternoon, there were no rules. No obligations. As far as everyone in Trumpet Manor was concerned, Melody was still holed up in Mr Pizzicato's music studio practising piano scales for the six hundredth time that day. She had just under two hours before she had to race back to the school to meet Royce, who had never arrived to pick her up later than three twenty-nine.

Melody's jaw dropped at the colourful sights as she walked deeper into Town Square. Crowds queued by the food trucks. Buskers dotted the perimeter of the square: jugglers, cartoonists, painters, didgeridoo players, magicians, saxophonists. She wandered closer, drawn in by their bright costumes and amazing skills.

Her stomach grumbled as she passed a food truck serving kebabs. The line was so long it wrapped around the square like a snake. Melody let person after person go ahead of her while she patted down her pockets in search of loose coins. But there was none, and no notes either, and nothing clinking in the bottom of her backpack. Unsurprising, really, as the Trumpets rarely paid for anything with cash.

Sighing, Melody left the line and made her way deeper into a crowd of people forming around a busker singing in the centre of the square. She couldn't see much but she could hear the strum of a guitar and a girl's voice that was gentle and full of lightness, like it might wrap around Melody and lift her feet off the ground.

She wriggled through the crowd for a better look. The busker wore faded denim overalls and was perched on a tiny wooden stool, swaying as she strummed the guitar and tapped her sneakers — which were ripped around the edges and revealed her big toes — to the beat. Her long, fiery red hair was braided into a thick plait that cascaded over one shoulder. A scruffy-looking white terrier with muddy paws lay at her side, dozing in the warm sun.

The girl finished performing and everyone clapped. A few people threw coins into the empty guitar case on the concrete in front of her. Most didn't.

As the crowd moved on, Melody walked forward, keeping her cap down low, and dropped down to pat the scruffy little dog.

'Wait, I've got more!' the busker cried out to the departing crowd. She leaped to her feet. 'Don't leave yet. I've saved the best till last, I promise. A new song, just for you all.'

But people continued to walk away, chowing into their kebabs and pizzas.

Shaking her head, the busker plonked back onto her stool and swung her guitar strap around her neck. She began to play, and still no one stopped or turned around. But then she opened her mouth and her voice, soft, husky and beautiful, drew the crowd back to her.

'*Just once*,' the girl sang, her eyes closed, '*Just once I'd like to be, in the kind of place that's in my head, the perfect place for me.*'

Melody stood up a little straighter. Was she hallucinating with hunger after skipping lunch? Or was this flame-haired busker really singing lines from her private notebook?

By now, the crowd was smiling in admiration. Even the scruffy little dog had woken up and was wagging his tail.

Melody thought she must be imagining it. No one had ever read her scribblings. She'd never shown a soul. Not even Mr Pizzicato.

Yet there was no denying it: the busker was singing her poem.

Where it's all okay,
And it's all alright,
And nothing is a pain.
Where the sun's not too hot,
The clouds aren't too grey,
And no one hates the rain.

10.

Clementine the busker

Everyone clapped and cheered as the busker sang the final note. She jumped to her feet to give a comical curtsy. Her dog barked, still wagging his tail.

'Thanking you, Battyville!' the girl said, holding up her guitar. 'If you're new here, I'm Clementine and this is my best friend, Moe.' The dog barked again. 'We're here often — same spot, different times. Tell your family, tell your friends, tell your enemies. Just tell people. Thanking you again, Battyville!'

The crowd gave her another round of applause and this time they swarmed to throw money into the guitar case.

Melody waited for the crowd to thin out, her teeth grinding while Clementine's new fans asked for hugs, photos and pats of Moe the dog. Eventually, she was the last person left. Moe glared at Melody, but Clementine didn't seem to realise she still had company. She poured the money into her backpack, then popped the guitar into its case and strapped it onto the back of a green tandem bicycle with rainbow streamers that was leaning against a nearby pole.

'Oh,' she said, finally noticing Melody standing behind her. 'Howdy there. Did you like the show? I suppose you're after a photograph or autograph?'

'I did like the show. Until you stole my words.'

Clementine froze, then faked a gasp. 'Steal? Me? I would never.'

Melody pointed to the sauce-stained brown leather-bound notebook peeking out of the straw basket hitched onto the back of the bicycle. 'That's mine. I'd know it anywhere.'

'No, no, that's my notebook. My very special book. Mine, all mine.'

'Oh, really?' Melody raised an eyebrow. 'If we look at whose initials are scribbled on the front, and the words filling the pages inside, the facts will suggest otherwise.'

'Facts? Is this an inquisition? Do I need to call a lawyer?' Clementine laughed. 'Go home. Build a fort. Collect stamps. Play with your friends.'

Melody stepped in front of Clementine's bicycle.

'Seriously,' Clementine continued, 'don't you have something better to do than harass a lowly busker trying to feed herself? This is a free country.'

'But that book isn't free. It belongs to me and you know it. Look at the first page. You go to the Battyville Elite School For Musically Gifted Children, do you? And your initials are M T for Melody Trumpet?'

'As a matter of fact they ...' Clementine's eyes widened. 'Wait, you're Melody Trumpet? As in ... *the* Trumpets. I thought you were a myth. Where have you been hiding all these years?'

'Um ...' Melody stammered. She wanted to run away to avoid getting in trouble. But she wanted her notebook back even more. 'Yes, I'm Melody Trumpet.'

'Well, right on!' Clementine cheered. 'You hear that, Moe? We're in the company of a genius. I can't believe it. A Trumpet! The richest and most talented family in Battyville. At *my* gig. I'm, like, famous by association or something. Sing us a song! Play something on the guitar! Wow us with your musical prowess!'

This was exactly why her parents had kept her away from strangers over the years, Melody realised.

'Yes, I'm a Trumpet,' she said, her voice trembling. 'As in *the* Trumpets. And we'll take you for everything you've got for stealing my notebook. Now give it back and I'll ... I'll be on my way.' She paused. 'Please.'

74

'A simple, "No thanks, I don't feel like singing today" would have sufficed,' Clementine said. She clicked her tongue. 'As for taking me for everything I've got — I'm afraid you and the all-powerful Trumpets are in for a disappointment.' She gestured to the bicycle, her guitar and Moe. 'That's my whole life right there, minus a few shabby clothes and a book or two. Just make sure you take Moe for a long walk by the lagoon every day otherwise he'll get skittish. Oh, and he has a refined palate. His favourite food is the five-cheese croissant from the patisserie around the corner. They toss out the leftovers at the end of the day so they don't cost us a cent. Which is lucky because I don't have many of those. So go on — clear me out. Take it all.'

Moe growled a warning, but Melody didn't move. She was thinking about her private wing at Trumpet Manor compared with Clementine's bike, guitar and a dog.

Clementine shrugged and adjusted her overalls. 'Okay, time's up. Guess you're not into stealing. The truth is, neither am I. But, you know what? Finding something and borrowing it for free from a rich family with no intention of giving it back anytime soon is a different story!'

She scooped Moe up in her arms and popped him into the bike basket. 'Tuck those paws in, boy — it's going to be a quick getaway!'

'You can't do this! Stop!' Melody shouted.

Clementine swung one leg over the bicycle. Moe barked from the back, a warning that Melody was still there.

'I'm truly sorry, kid!' Clementine called out as she pedalled off, streamers blowing in the wind. 'Finders keepers! Thanking you! Thanking you with all my heart!'

11.

Secrets between friends

Melody plopped down on a wooden bench in the square and traced a jagged crack in the seat with her fingertip. What was she supposed to do next?

Principal Sharp was making preparations for the Debut Gala.

Her parents were close to throttling her.

Mr Pizzicato's nerves had frayed until they split.

And now a busker called Clementine had stolen her most treasured possession: her notebook.

'*Where the sun's not too hot,*' she murmured, too forlorn to cringe as her voice swayed in and out of tune. '*The clouds aren't too grey, and no one hates the rain ...*'

'Blimey, does your voice need a tune-up or what?'

Startled, Melody looked up to see Freddie Bloom standing in front of her, his skateboard tucked under one arm.

'Lucky the words sound alright,' he added.

Melody blushed, wondering how much he had heard. 'Just practising. What are you doing here?'

'I followed you.' He beamed. 'Isn't that obvious?'

Melody leaped to her feet and swung her backpack over her shoulders. 'Well, you shouldn't have. How long have you been here?'

'Not too long.' He shrugged. 'Fine, twenty minutes. Fine, over an hour. Fine, I've been here the whole time. I saw that busker steal your book, and I know you're keeping another secret. You can't sing.'

'I was just being silly,' Melody said with a fake laugh. 'I'm a Trumpet. Of course I can sing.'

'My mistake. You're a Trumpet who can't sing *well*.'

Melody cleared her throat. 'Maybe I sound so good that I don't want to make everyone else feel bad so I pretend I can't sing.'

'Maybe ...' Freddie said with an unconvinced look.

Melody hated lying. Her parents made her do it all day, every day, and it was exhausting. She sighed and slumped back onto the bench. 'My parents have managed to keep my miserable lack of musical talent a secret from the town — from the world — for years. But after just a few hours on my own, I meet you, lose everything that's important to me, and reveal the life-ruining secret that I'm just an ordinary nobody. I really am as hopeless as my parents say. And I guess now you'll tell everyone our big secret.'

'Hey!' He sat down next to her. 'I said I'd never tell anyone your secrets, Melody Trumpet. And that's two now.' He pretended to lock his lips again and threw his imaginary key over his shoulder. 'Remember? I reckon this makes us friends.'

'We are?' Melody wanted to trust Freddie. She'd never had a friend before. The only problem was, she didn't know how this whole friendship thing worked. 'Does that mean you need to tell me something about you now, to even it out?'

'Ask me anything,' he said. 'My favourite colour? Green — love the bow by the way. My favourite footy team? The Battyville Bulldogs obviously, because they're the best — and anyone who says otherwise is a traitor. My favourite breakfast? Waffles, ice-cream and strawberry topping. What else do you want to know?'

'Why would you keep my secret?' Melody asked. 'Everyone else at school would dob me in to Principal Sharp without a second thought. It's a huge scandal — you could sell the story and make a fortune. You'd be famous.'

'I don't give a rat's tail about fame,' Freddie said. 'And I'm not like everyone else at school. They'd be the first ones to tell you that — if you ever slummed it with us, that is.'

Melody wrinkled her nose. She'd overheard Mr Bloom telling Miss Sprinkles more than once about his eldest's son's meteoric rise at the Battyville Elite School For Musically Gifted Children. 'I thought you were top of the class? Perfect grades, destined for greatness — all that?'

Freddie snorted. 'You think those snobs care about my grades, or the fact I can play the piano by ear while blindfolded?'

'Now you're showing off.'

'They only care about prestige and riches. Everything I haven't got.' He shrugged. 'You'd probably fit right in.'

'That's not fair,' Melody said. 'I'm the outsider.'

'You're a *Trumpet*. Your parents' faces are all over the walls of the school. You're who everyone aspires to be. I'm on a scholarship. I don't have nice clothes, and I share a bedroom with my six-year-old brother and five-year-old sister. Doesn't matter how hard I try, how many awards I win, everyone always sees me as second-class.'

Melody swallowed. She'd had no idea.

'You don't have to say anything,' Freddie added, tugging at his faded jacket that Melody now realised was probably a hand-me-down. 'That's just the way it is.

But it doesn't help that my dad works in the dirt for the richest family in town.'

'Your father loves that garden,' Melody said. 'I don't think I've ever seen a weed in my life.'

Freddie chuckled. 'He is obsessed. *Do what you love* — that's what he says.' He gently elbowed Melody. 'So you *really* can't sing?'

She shook her head.

'What about playing an instrument? The piano?'

'Can't play.'

'Guitar?'

'Nope.'

'Not even the *trumpet*?'

She managed a watery laugh. 'Not even that. Pathetic, right?'

'No. Just … surprising.' Freddie squinted up at the sun, before flashing Melody a warm smile. 'What are you good at then?'

'I'm not good at anything.'

'Come on. Everyone's good at something.'

'I'm not! I only know what I like doing.'

'Even better. What's that?'

'Writing. I love writing.' Melody sighed. 'But that busker stole my notebook. It's everything to me.'

Freddie stood up. 'Then we've got to get it back.'

'How?'

He held out his hand for Melody to grasp onto, and pulled her to her feet. 'That I don't know ... yet.'

'Freddie?' she began, straightening the baseball cap.

'Yeah?'

'You saw the busker, right? Clementine? Did you like her songs?'

'Sure, especially the last one. Everyone liked it.'

'That was mine. My words, anyway.'

Freddie's eyes widened. 'Really? Well, I liked it. A lot.'

'Oh ... thanks,' Melody said, blushing. 'It was nothing.'

'Hey, it was something! No more lies between us from now on, only secrets,' he continued. 'Promise?'

She nodded, 'Promise,' and shook his outstretched hand. 'Now I'd better get back to school before my driver arrives. I'm running late.'

His eyes widened. 'You have a driver? Nice. The cap looks good by the way,' he added. 'You know what? You can keep it, Melody Trumpet.'

'Thanks, Freddie Bloom.'

12.

An unfortunate misunderstanding

Mrs Trumpet poked her head out of the walk-in pantry and waved at Mr Trumpet with her pointy red nails. 'Yoo-hoo! In here! Quickly!' she whispered. 'We need to talk. *Now.*'

Mr Trumpet looked at her in shock. 'Are you mad, Viola? Why can't we just go back to our wing and ...' His stomach growled before he could finish the sentence. 'Ohhh, fine.' He hurried into the pantry and closed the door. 'It's very cramped in here.'

His stomach growled again. 'Nope, this won't do.' He pulled down a loaf of sliced bread off a shelf, and sniffed around for some toppings. His oversized stomach, which strained against his suspenders, knocked a row of jars and cans onto the floor with a crash.

Mrs Trumpet sucked in a breath. 'It's the child, Barry. Something's up. She hasn't mentioned her class today with Mr Pizzicato, and Royce said she was late to arrive at the limousine this afternoon for the first time ever. But the most curious thing of all ... she's smiling. She never smiles, the miserable little flea.'

'What? Late? Smiling?' Mr Trumpet spluttered, choking on his sandwich.

Mrs Trumpet pursed her lips together. 'She shouldn't be smiling at all. I discarded that rotten old notebook the other day so she'd keep her focus on the Debut Gala. This is most curious. There must be something she's not telling us ... Come with me, my sticky cinnamon bun. Let's investigate.'

Mr and Mrs Trumpet eased out of the pantry, tiptoed across the grand foyer, up the staircase to Melody's wing, and peeked through the door.

Melody lay on her stomach on the carpet watching cartoons, her bare feet dancing in the air. She chomped on a sandwich, giggling as honey dripped down her chin.

'See!' Mrs Trumpet hissed, elbowing Mr Trumpet. 'Laughter! Completely out of the ordinary.'

'Very suspicious,' Mr Trumpet agreed, his eyes narrowing.

'Unless ...' Mrs Trumpet grabbed Mr Trumpet's hand and dragged him back down to the kitchen. She held the pantry door open and gestured to him to go back inside.

He wrinkled his nose. 'Darling Viola ... just tell me here. Small spaces aren't my speciality and I've eaten enough bread.'

'What if the child's ... *happy*? Oh!' Mrs Trumpet gasped. 'You know what this means?'

'She likes cartoons? Or honey sandwiches? Speaking of which, maybe I could squeeze in another sandwich or two ...'

'No, you silly sausage. It means things must *finally* be going well with Mr Pizzicato. Oh, my bean burrito, our dramas are over.'

He beamed at her. 'We knew this day would come, my squidgy little tortellini. Laughter, smiling, relaxed — all signs of a child who has found her talent.'

* * *

Melody was now curled up on the bed, flicking through the channels on the television.

'No smile,' Mrs Trumpet whispered in Mr Trumpet's ear, although her idea of whispering was so loud it could help ships find their way home in the night. 'Or is that a frown? It looks like a frown. Maybe I was wrong ... maybe I imagined the whole thing.'

Melody waved at her parents in the doorway. 'Ah, I can hear you. What's going on?'

'Oh!' said Mrs Trumpet, taking a step forward. 'Well, when I popped past earlier you seemed so blissful. And now ...'

Melody nibbled on her nail. 'I'm just watching TV. Or is that banned too now?'

'No. Unless Mr Pizzicato has banned it? If he has, you must turn it off immediately.' Mrs Trumpet's voice grew increasingly high-pitched. Mr Trumpet touched her gently on the arm and she paused, pursing her lips. 'My apologies. Melody, our love, can we chat with you for a second?'

Our love? Melody thought to herself. 'Ah, sure.'

'Lovely. So, ah, how are things ... ah, proceeding in the lead-up to the Gala?' Mrs Trumpet put on a sickly sweet voice as she plopped her rotund bottom down on the bed.

Melody's jaw tightened. She hadn't spoken to her mother since she'd thrown her notebook into the rubbish bin. How did she think Melody was going after that?

'I'm fine. Just hanging out,' she said with a shrug.

'And how are lessons with Mr Pizzicato? Are things moving in the right direction? I hear their Royal Highnesses are extremely excited about your debut.'

'Things are ... Well, I'm happy with how things are going,' said Melody.

It was only a half-lie. She was devastated by the loss of her notebook, and petrified about the upcoming Debut Gala, but she had something else to be happy about. Her first ever friend, Freddie Bloom. Melody's mouth creased into a smile.

'See, Barry,' Mrs Trumpet said, clinging to Mr Trumpet's solid upper arm. 'It's true. She's happy!'

'So classes with Mr Pizzicato are different?' Mr Trumpet probed. 'Maybe you're both doing things in a new way — a way that you haven't tried before?'

Melody thought of Mr Pizzicato flopped on the couch, and his announcement that he was leaving on a spontaneous holiday to a tropical island.

'Yes, things are definitely different,' she said.

Mrs Trumpet squealed and clapped her hands. 'Wonderful, child. Well, keep it up. This new way seems to be working — the beam on your face says it all. I knew Mr Pizzicato would come through for us in the end. It only took years ...'

'Viola ...' Mr Trumpet warned.

'I'll be quiet,' Mrs Trumpet said. She huddled closer to Melody on the bed. 'Although ... I can't resist! Would you like to try on your Claudette Rought gown again to celebrate? It looks so scrumptious.'

'Ah, I don't think so,' said Melody.

'Why not?' Mrs Trumpet huffed. 'You'll be the most spectacular person there — other than me and the Princess of course! I know, why don't you give us a sneak-peek performance of what you've been working on with Mr Pizzicato?'

'I, for one, cannot wait to hear it,' added Mr Trumpet. 'Is it conducting, like your old pop, Melody?' He beamed, no doubt imagining her tiny figure in front of an orchestra.

'Or opera?' chimed in Mrs Trumpet. 'Tell me it's singing, child. Or the cello, like your great-grandmother? I'm so thrilled at the possibilities I could explode.'

'It's …' Melody's cheeks burned. 'It's … Mr Pizzicato said …'

Her stomach churned. She had to tell her parents the truth. She'd hated all the lies she'd been forced into — and she couldn't keep it up. Especially not a lie as big as Mr Pizzicato quitting his job right before the Debut Gala. 'Um … the truth is —'

'Hold that thought, Melody!' Mrs Trumpet said, disappearing out the door.

She returned with three sapphire-blue feather boas from the locked display cabinet in the grand foyer. *The Untouchables*, Melody called them, because they were worth an undisclosed amount and no one was ever allowed to touch them. The feathers were from a rare species of peacock found in the tropical forests of a tiny island on the other side of the world, so the boas were only allowed to be admired from a safe distance. Until now.

Mrs Trumpet draped one boa around Melody's neck, and looped another around Mr Trumpet's. Then she popped on some music — from her own platinum-selling album, of course — and took Melody's hand in hers. 'This triumph deserves a celebration!' she said, and waltzed Melody around the wing, too caught up in her own excitement and the sound of her voice on the album to realise Melody hadn't told them anything.

But as her mother swept Melody along in her arms, lifting her, spinning her, laughter escaped both of their lips. Real laughter.

Is this what it feels like to be part of something? Melody thought. *Part of a real family?*

As Mrs Trumpet twirled her from one side of the room to the other, Melody pushed the truth down so deep that it wouldn't slip out. She told herself there was still time to confess to her parents that Mr Pizzicato had abandoned her. But for now she just wanted to enjoy the bubbly, fizzy happiness in her stomach.

A feeling like she belonged.

13.

Through the hidden passage

Royce stopped the limousine outside the secret entrance to the Battyville Elite School For Musically Gifted Children. He turned off the engine and drew in a deep breath. They sat in silence for a few moments. She knew what he was thinking. Where was Mr Pizzicato?

Day after day, year after year, Mr Pizzicato had waited for Melody at the entrance with a steaming hot chocolate in one hand and a gingernut biscuit in the other. But he wasn't there today. It seemed yesterday hadn't been just a strange dream as Melody had hoped.

'No Mr Pizzicato this morning, Miss Trumpet?' Royce said.

'He must be inside, setting up the ... ah ... the instruments for the ... ah ... the ... thing. The rehearsal! We're extra busy today.'

Fibbing to Royce didn't feel right, but Melody hoped against hope that Mr Pizzicato might be playing the most excruciating game of hide and seek ever. Maybe if she wished hard enough, he would magically appear inside the studio.

'So ... bye then,' she said to Royce, forcing a fake smile.

'Wait!' He got out of the limousine to open the door for her. 'I should come in with you and check everything is okay.'

'Why wouldn't everything be okay?' Melody asked, hoping her voice didn't sound too high-pitched. 'Mr Pizzicato is in inside, then I'll be inside, then we'll both be inside, then ... then ... everything will continue to be okay inside ... Okay?'

'Ah, yes, well, I suppose so.'

'I'm sure you have a very busy morning ahead, Royce. I know the way. I've done this thousands of times. You know that.'

'I'll wait here, just in case.'

'*Royce*.'

'*Miss Trumpet*.'

Melody folded her arms. 'I'm not a little kid.'

'But your parents —'

'Will be fine with it. Ask them.'

This was a gamble and Melody knew it.

'Excellent idea. I'll do just that.'

Melody bit her lip as Royce whipped out his phone and called the manor.

'It's ringing out,' he told her.

Melody peeked at his watch. 'Of course it is. It's eight o'clock. Mother will be at yoga, then brunch with the opera alumni. Father will be asleep.'

Royce sighed. 'Fine. I will be back here at three twenty-nine sharp. Yesterday's tardiness was a no-no. If you're so much as a second late —'

'I'll be a second early,' Melody told him. 'See you this afternoon.'

Backpack bouncing on her shoulders, Melody walked through the secret entrance into the secret passage. Now she had to remember which way to turn to get to Mr Pizzicato's private music studio. She was used to following her teacher through the passage each morning in a sleepy daze.

Melody wandered along, stopping to peek through the tiny glass windows that allowed a glimpse into the classrooms below. The secret passage was so high above everything that no one had any inkling they were being watched, or that the passage even existed.

In one classroom a single boy and his teacher were playing a duet on the piano, their long spindly fingers flying between the pages of sheet music and the black and white keys. In another, three girls, each about Melody's age, giggled as they played their violins. The tallest girl stood on top of her desk and waved her violin bow in the air like she was casting a spell. Melody pressed her nose to the glass, watching as the other two clambered onto their desks and copied their friend, then they all cracked up laughing. She walked on.

Surely she had almost reached the studio by now? She didn't remember it taking this long to get there, but she'd always had Mr Pizzicato for company in the past.

Finally, she came to the studio door. She brushed her fingers over the scratches in the wood that she'd seen thousands of times. Mr Pizzicato often moaned about the scratches but Melody thought they added character. She fumbled in her jacket pocket for the key Mr Pizzicato had given her, and pushed it into the keyhole. Then, for the first time ever, she turned the brass doorknob and opened the door.

The room was in darkness, except for a sliver of light coming from the hallway.

'Mr P?' Melody whispered. 'Are you here?' She fumbled around in the black, her fingertips finding the light switch. 'Mr Pizzicato?' she said again, voice cracking.

Pale yellow light flooded the room. It was empty. The instruments were lined up or packed neatly away.

The cushions on the couch had been plumped up. Everything was in its place. And there was no sign at all of Mr Pizzicato.

Melody walked to the grand piano and sat down on the leather seat. Her right thumb pushed down on the piano's middle C key, and it rang clear and bright, teasing her with the promise of a perfect musical scale. Encouraged, Melody brought both hands to the piano's glossy white keys. Her fingers stumbled from key to key, creating a jerky, stuttering sound. Melody cringed. It wasn't exactly the smooth run she had hoped for.

She picked up a guitar and strummed its strings, but they shuddered at her touch. One string vibrated so hard it snapped with a loud twang! She quickly put it back in its case.

Sighing, Melody stared at the calendar on Mr Pizzicato's wall with its big red crosses. The days were disappearing and she had no idea how she was going to get herself out of this mess. And with the half-lie to her parents, she'd dug herself in even deeper.

Soon Principal Sharp, the city of Battyville, the entire world — maybe even alien life on other planets — would know that Melody Trumpet was a sham. Her parents would lose their iconic status, their manor, everything that was so important to them, and there wasn't anything she could do about it.

But Melody wasn't one to call it quits. She always tried her best, even when her best seemed to be the worst. She racked her brains for ideas — but still nothing came to her. All she could think about was what she was going to perform at the Debut Gala now that Mr Pizzicato wasn't here to teach her.

She needed help. A music whiz.

A friend.

Melody knew just the person to ask.

* * *

Armed with some old sheet music and a pen, Melody went back to the secret passage and peeked down into classroom after classroom. Finally, she came to one that was a flurry of students and colours and movement. There was no teacher at the front of the room. Two girls threw a tennis ball over the other students' heads, and a group of boys were huddled in a corner playing cards. A girl wearing a pirate hat was scribbling *I love farts* on the blackboard. Melody laughed. What *was* this class? It looked a lot more fun than her sessions with Mr Pizzicato.

Then she saw him. Freddie. He was sitting cross-legged on his desk, flipping through a comic book. Every now and then he'd laugh out loud. He wriggled around on the hard desk, no doubt uncomfortable, then jumped down onto the carpet and lay on his back to read the comic.

At first his face was blocked from view by the comic book, but eventually it dropped onto his chest. When it did, he caught sight of Melody peering through the tiny window near the ceiling. She beamed and gave a wave, then immediately wondered if she should have ducked out of view. But he gave her a thumbs-up in reply, his eyes wide in excitement.

Melody dropped to her knees and scribbled a note for Freddie on the sheet music, giving him directions on how to meet her at the secret entrance at recess. She folded the paper into an aeroplane and whispered, 'Sorry, Mr Pizzicato, but it's an emergency.'

She pushed the paper aeroplane through a small grey vent at her feet. Once it was through the tight gap, she pressed her nose to the glass again, gesturing to Freddie to look up. He did, but nothing happened. He cocked his head to the side, confused. Still nothing. Melody bit her lip. This wasn't the plan. This wasn't how it was meant to go at all.

Suddenly the aeroplane burst out of the vent and into Freddie's classroom, floating and dancing on the ceiling like magic.

Freddie sprinted to the front of the class and plucked the aeroplane from the air seconds before its sharp nose made contact with the carpet. Grinning, he scurried back to his desk and slid into his chair, shooing away nosy classmates, and slipped the aeroplane into his backpack.

Success!

At recess, Melody found Freddie waiting for her at the entrance to the secret passage with his skateboard.

'That was wild!' he blurted with excitement, waving the paper aeroplane in her face.

Melody agreed it was pretty cool but there was no time for chit-chat. After a quick check left and right, she snuck Freddie inside the secret passage and led him up to the soundproofed music studio.

'This is awesome,' he said. 'And this passageway has been here all this time, right above our heads? Wow!' His voice trailed off as they reached the studio door. 'Wait, where's your teacher? Won't they freak out if they see me with you?'

'He's gone. Quit. Bailed.'

Freddie's eyebrows shot up in surprise. 'Just before the Debut Gala?'

'He gave up. I don't blame him. It's kind of why you're here though ...'

'Really?' He cocked his head to the side. 'Another secret! And another whopper!'

She nodded and turned the door handle.

From the moment Freddie stepped into the studio, everything felt different to Melody, like someone had turned the lights on in the room for the first time. For so many years it had just been her and Mr Pizzicato in the studio, her tiny frame and his spindly body barely filling the space. Freddie was no bigger than she was, but his voice was loud and happy, and his smile was wide and gap-toothed.

He ran to examine each instrument, his jaw dropping at their quality. A slight twinge of jealousy pulsated in Melody's chest when she saw the ease with which he handled them all, from the trumpet to the violin, but she banished the feeling. She reminded herself that she was glad to have a friend, and seeing Freddie's glee made her feel happy about the studio for the first time. Usually she dreaded the place and hated the instruments, but watching Freddie play them brought her joy.

As he shredded on an electric guitar, Melody glanced at the calendar behind him again. She imagined dressing Freddie up as her for the Debut Gala. A jet-black wig, her gown from Claudette Rouge's and he'd be perfect. The thought of his wild curly hair peeking out from beneath the wig made her laugh.

'What's so funny?' he asked, his fingers sliding up and down the neck of the guitar.

Melody smirked. 'Never mind.'

Freddie put down the guitar and walked over to an enormous gold tuba. 'Look at this beauty. You really don't wanna play any of these instruments? Don't you need to practise for the Gala?'

'That's the problem. I don't have a performance worked out, and I don't have a teacher now either. I was hoping you might be able to help? I don't even have my notebook any more to write down all my —'

'Wait, your notebook — that's it!' Freddie punched the air. 'That busker girl in Town Square turned your words into songs. You *are* musical ... but it's all trapped in that notebook.'

'That girl — Clementine — stole it. I can't just magically make it reappear.'

'No, but you could track her down at Town Square again.' He broke into a grin. 'I've got a better idea: *we* could track her down at Town Square again.'

'Shouldn't you be rehearsing for the Gala too?'

'Nah, I nailed my performance ages ago.' He cringed as he realised what he'd said. 'Er, sorry. Besides, you might need someone with you to distract the busker while you get your notebook back.'

'I guess so.'

'Let's do it. And maybe that dog will be there too.' He grinned. 'I've gotta run but I'll meet you outside the secret entrance at lunchtime. Deal?'

Melody nodded, butterflies fluttering in her stomach. She was nervous about venturing out in public again, but after lying to her parents, and no prospects at all for her performance at the Debut Gala, she had to do something. Besides, she'd broken so many rules now that she'd lost track of how much trouble she would be in if she got caught.

So that lunchtime, Melody plopped Freddie's cap on her head again and returned with him to Town Square to try to catch Clementine in the act.

'You just missed her,' one of Clementine's adoring fans told Melody and Freddie that first afternoon.

The next day, they tried again. Again, they were out of luck.

'She did a sunrise performance today,' a starstruck local told them. 'She's an enigma that one. And what a talent! Her newest songs are just wonderful.'

Freddie elbowed Melody. 'That's your stuff,' he whispered.

Melody sighed. 'Maybe we should give up?'

'Maybe.' He readjusted her cap. 'Or here's an idea: maybe we just try again tomorrow.'

14.

A new plan

Melody tugged at the baseball cap, pulling it down even further as she and Freddie snuck through the school grounds.

'Don't worry, no one suspects a thing,' Freddie said, striding ahead. 'But hurry, we don't want to miss her. Today's the day, I can feel it!'

'It's out of our control,' puffed Melody, trying to keep up. 'It all comes down to when *she* decides to perform.'

'Hey, she had long red hair, right?'

'Yep.'

'In a plait? Kinda wavy?'

'Um, I think so.'

'And was her bike green? And a tandem?'

'I think so ... Why all the questions?'

Freddie spun around to face Melody. 'Because she's right there!' He pointed to a girl sitting on a bench in the school's rotunda. 'And look, her pooch is there too.'

Melody gasped and came to a halt. 'Clementine's here? *Why?* She couldn't get away from me fast enough the other day. Something's not right ...'

'I have no idea, but let's find out,' Freddie said, and he linked his arm with Melody's and gently led her across the grass towards the rotunda.

Melody's jaw tightened as they marched closer. She searched for what she might say to Clementine but nothing came to mind.

Moe barked, causing Clementine to spin around. Her eyes widened when she saw Melody and Freddie, then she grinned. 'Well, well, well, is this fate or what?'

'Why are you here?' asked Melody, hands on her hips.

'I want to talk to you. I was just trying to come up with a plan to bust you out of that school.'

'How did you know where to find me?'

'You told me, remember?' Clementine impersonated her: *'I'm Melody Trumpet and I go to the Battyville Elite School For Musically Gifted Children*. Simple.'

'That was pretty good. She sounded just like you,' whispered Freddie.

Melody shot him a disapproving look.

'As luck would have it — and no judgey-wudgey faces from you two — I happen to be banned from being within a five-hundred-metre radius of the school for toilet-papering the car park. Oops.'

'That was *you*? People talked about that for weeks.' Freddie laughed, then cocked his head to one side. 'But I don't get it. Why's that lucky?'

'Because being banned from the premises forced me to hang out in the rotunda here to plan my big entrance — and look who happens to stroll past? Melody Trumpet, just the gal I need to see.'

'No, *I* need to see you,' Melody said. 'I want my notebook back.'

'Ahh, the notebook.' Clementine nodded. 'That's why I'm here too.'

'It is?'

Clementine picked up her bicycle, wheeled it down the steps of the rotunda onto the grass and patted the second seat. 'Hop on.'

'Yeah, right!' Melody said, arms folded over her chest. 'I'm not getting on that deathtrap. I'll just take my notebook and then we'll be on our way.'

Clementine laughed. 'The tandem's perfectly safe. There's no need to get all prickly. And I'm going to give you the notebook — soon. I promise.'

Melody looked to Freddie for a clue about what to do. He shrugged.

'But I need to show you something important first,' Clementine said. 'Come on. It won't take long. Well, not too long.' She passed Melody a chipped silver bike helmet. 'Safety first!'

Melody slipped the helmet onto her head over the baseball cap. 'I don't know … this feels ridiculous …'

Tongue sticking out in concentration, Clementine tightened the helmet's straps.

'Ouch, that hurts,' Melody said, squirming.

'Quit complaining. That's not the girl I know!'

'You don't know me at all,' Melody told her.

'Sure I do. Your name is Melody Trumpet, you like writing, you're friends with this young chap —'

'Freddie!' he chimed in.

'You're friends with Freddie, and you're a nice person, if not a bit grumpy. You also have neat handwriting, enjoy using commas, and have lots of thoughts about lots of things.'

Melody looked unimpressed. 'So you've read my notebook. Big deal.'

'You also like choc-mint ice-cream.'

Choc-mint was Melody's favourite flavour but she was certain she'd never written a poem about it. 'How do you know that?'

'I have a knack for these sorts of things,' Clementine said. 'Well, that and you smudged some chocolate on the pages. I had a cautious sniff while reading.'

'So you read … everything?'

Clementine nodded and looked at Melody with warm eyes. 'I did. Once I started, I couldn't stop. And after reading your notebook, I feel like we have a lot in common.'

'Oh really?'

'Sure! We couldn't have had more different beginnings, it's true. You, raised in a mega-mansion with famous parents and all the pressure in the world. And me, an orphan who ran away from her shady aunt and uncle, and was rescued from the streets by Mumma Rose. But neither of us have a loving family and people we can count on.'

Melody stared. She'd expected to feel furious by Clementine's theft and her betrayal of Melody's privacy, but instead her soft, kind tone made her feel understood.

'You hopping on or what?' Clementine asked.

'Okay,' Melody said, clambering onto the second seat. 'But just so you know, I've never done this before.'

Clementine turned around. 'What? Ridden a bike?'

Melody nodded.

'*Never*?'

'Never.'

'No worries, I'll do all the pedalling,' Clementine said. 'You just hold on tight. Moe will keep you company back there.'

Right on cue the pooch jumped into the basket behind Melody.

Freddie held up his skateboard. 'I'm coming too.'

'No way,' Clementine said, holding up her hand. 'I can't be responsible for both of you.'

'You won't even notice I'm here,' he insisted. 'I'll be like the invisible man, a ghost, a shadow —'

'Fine, you can come,' Clementine said. 'But I'm going to live to regret this. Okay, let's go!'

Clementine pushed off and started pedalling, and Moe woofed with delight. Freddie jumped on his skateboard and raced alongside the tandem bicycle.

They were on their way.

* * *

The air whipped about Melody's hair as Clementine pedalled through the streets of Battyville. Melody wrapped her fingers tightly around the second set of handlebars, but her feet dangled just above the pedals so she couldn't help. She peeked over her shoulder to watch Freddie gliding behind them on his skateboard.

Melody tried to track where Clementine was taking them, but was too distracted by the sights and smells as they sailed along the winding bicycle paths. On Jupiter Lane they passed a row of trees bursting with colourful and fragrant flowers. On the corner of Spy Street and Boffin Avenue, a man was setting up a stall with a sign that read: *Jewellery for sale*. Clementine pedalled on, until she reached Dreamers Parade. Melody was captivated by the bustling people, the fairy lights twinkling on the trees, the flashing neon signs.

'Hold on,' Clementine puffed. 'Hill.'

It was a steep climb and Clementine's legs pushed down harder and harder to keep them moving. Moe barked in motivation. Freddie had to get off his skateboard and carry it up the hill, red and wheezing behind them. Frightened by the steep angle, Melody wanted to close her eyes but she forced herself to keep them open and soak everything in. This was life beyond Trumpet Manor — and she was finally getting to see it without a limousine window in the way.

Dreamers Parade became more and more narrow, winding around corners and through tunnels, and over the Battyville Bridge across the lagoon.

'Nearly there,' Clementine squeezed out between puffs.

This was another side to Battyville — one that Melody had never seen before. People strolled past wearing colourful flashy shirts that clashed with their pants, and layers of beaded necklaces. A group danced on the footpath to music bursting out of a speaker set up on the steps of a house. Melody even saw a young man rollerskating along the street with a python wrapped around his neck! She was so mesmerised she forgot she was supposed to be angry at Clementine for stealing her notebook.

The tandem bicycle stopped outside a tall, narrow terraced house. Next door to the left, an old woman with purple hair sat at an easel on the balcony, painting a canvas with a rainbow of watercolours. Next door to the right, a muscular ballet dancer in a unitard and leg warmers was stretching his powerful legs along the rail that led up to the front door, while playing cards with two girls in matching tutus.

'Here we are,' Clementine said to Melody and Freddie, waving to her neighbours. The artist saluted with her paintbrush and the dancers called out a hello. 'Welcome to Dreamers Parade.'

She wheeled the bicycle to the middle terrace house and propped it against the wall.

'You don't need to lock it up inside?' Melody asked. 'What if someone steals it?'

'People don't steal around here,' Clementine scoffed, scooping Moe out of the basket and plopping him onto the ground. 'They might borrow something for a while, but things always find their way back to their rightful owners.'

Melody smirked. 'Like someone's notebook, perhaps?'

'Exactly.' Clementine grinned as she and Moe climbed up the steps to the front door. 'Coming?' she asked Melody and Freddie.

Melody looked at the dancers who were now pirouetting on the pavement in front of their building. 'Um ...'

Freddie, still breathless from the climb, gasped, 'Yes ... need ... water.'

'I just want my notebook,' Melody said.

'Perfect! Come on then!' Clementine clasped her hands together as Melody and Freddie joined her at the front door. 'Are you ready to visit The Workshop? Five sharp knocks and Mumma Rose will let us in. Anything less and the door stays locked.'

'Workshop?' asked Melody. 'Mumma Rose?'

Freddie was more to the point. 'You're not in a weird cult, are you?'

Clementine laughed. 'Weird? Yes. *Wonderfully weird*. But a cult? Absolutely not.'

Melody swallowed and stepped up to the door. She knocked twice, then froze, suddenly feeling very far from everything she knew at Trumpet Manor.

'Five,' Clementine whispered. 'You can count to five, can't you?'

Melody wrinkled her nose and rapped the door five times.

'Well, that's technically seven all up, but who's counting, right?' Clementine said as the door swung open to reveal a tall bony woman with pink hair cut in a pixie style, red spectacles and glitter on her cheekbones.

'Clementine,' the woman said, pulling her in for a hug.

'This is Mumma Rose,' Clementine said in a grand voice. 'She keeps an eye on things at The Workshop.'

Mumma Rose's eyes twinkled. 'What she's trying to say is, I'm the boss. My workshop, my rules.' She peered down at Melody and Freddie. 'And who are these two tiny people?'

'This is Freddie,' Clementine said, 'and this is Melody Trumpet — the girl I was telling you about. As in *the* Melody Trumpet.'

'I see. Are you someone from the television?' Mumma Rose asked, squinting at Melody. 'Because we don't have a television.'

It was the first time someone hadn't made a fuss when they heard the Trumpet name. Melody liked it.

'No, I'm just me,' she said.

'Then welcome.' Mumma Rose stepped aside and waved them into The Workshop.

Melody and Freddie traded nervous glances. What were they walking into?

15.

Welcome to The Workshop

They entered a room that was at least two storeys high, with three levels of bookshelves and thin balconies with wooden railings lining one of the walls. Enormous paintings, photographs and sculptures hung from the walls to its left and right. The windows were small and didn't give much light, but a lamp glowed in one corner, highlighting the clutter that covered nearly every metre of the floorboards. The fourth and final wall was blank. Pure white. Completely untouched.

Melody took a step closer, her fingertips grazing the empty wall. Her body twitched with the urge to fill it with words; to make it feel alive like the rest of the room.

A loud yawn followed by whispers came from a mezzanine floor high above them. Melody elbowed Freddie and directed his attention to the sound. They edged a little closer to each other, alone in the large space. Clementine had gone into the kitchen with Mumma Rose to fetch a jug of water, and Moe was curled up on a couch, already snoring.

'Is that a child?' a girl's voice murmured. She sounded grumpy.

A light and airy giggle, then a boy said, 'Of course it's a child, Allira. Two, in fact. A her and a him. You know, you were a child yourself mere years ago, sister dearest. Aww, look at the little poppets.'

'They don't look very friendly.'

'Shhh, I think you're scaring them,' the boy said.

'If they find me scary, they need to toughen up.'

Melody cleared her throat and dared to call up to the mezzanine. 'Hello?'

No reply, but she saw an older boy duck down behind the balcony.

Melody shrugged. 'Okay then ...' she said, her voice trembling, 'who's scared now?'

High-pitched giggles rattled around the room. 'She got us there, Allira, you have to admit,' the boy said. He peeked at them from above the railing and Melody saw a toothy smile and thin dreadlocks. 'Hi there!' he called, before disappearing again.

Suddenly, he yanked a wiry girl up by her collar so they were both standing in clear view. They looked identical, from their dreadlocks and deep brown complexions to their wiry limbs and their head-to-toe athletic gear.

'Say hello, Allira,' said the boy.

Allira gave them a small wave, then turned back to the boy. 'You couldn't just let me sleep in like you promised? Fine. If I have to get up, then Gaff's getting up too. Gaff, we have visitors!'

A tall man with a thin moustache popped up by her side. He was holding a burning wooden torch. 'Howdy,' he announced, then sipped from an *I love my mum* mug. He swished the liquid around his mouth, then spat it at the torch, sending red flames shooting into the air. He did it again, then gave a small bow before disappearing back behind the balcony.

'Fire-breathers — always gotta steal the show,' the boy called down to Melody and Freddie. 'I'm Slack, by the way.'

'I'm … I'm Melody,' she stammered, still stunned by the spectacle.

'And I'm Freddie!' Freddie added.

Slack wrapped an arm around the wiry girl. 'Nice to meet you. That was Gaff, and this is my twin, Allira. Although sometimes I wonder if we're even related. She's such a party pooper.'

Allira rolled her eyes. 'Fine! I'm coming down.'

114

She jumped up on top of the balcony railing, chin lifted and arms stretched wide, and swung her right leg back and forth, building up momentum. Melody gasped.

'Show-off,' drawled Slack, leaning on the railing next to his twin, a lopsided smirk at the corner of his mouth.

Allira winked at her brother, then dived off the railing. Her body coiled into a tight somersault before landing softly, knees bent, on the rug in front of Melody and Freddie.

Melody and Freddie clapped, their jaws dropped in delight.

Allira sucked in a breath, then stretched out her long, graceful arms to accept the applause.

'Every time,' Slack laughed, skipping down the stairs.

'That was incredible,' Melody said.

'No, that was Allira,' Slack said, sticking out his hand for Melody and Freddie to shake.

'I see the party has begun,' Mumma Rose said, entering the room on the shoulders of a short stocky woman with long flowing blonde hair and muscles nearly bursting out of her clothes.

Clementine trailed behind them, holding a jug of water, her mouth stretched into a grin at the sight of Melody's and Freddie's stunned faces.

'And they haven't even met our resident mime artist, magician, human statue or knife thrower yet, or seen Gaff on a pair of stilts,' added Slack with a laugh.

'Helga, pop me down by our guests, please,' Mumma Rose said. She held up a plate each of caramel slice and oatmeal biscuits as the blonde woman lifted her above her head five times, grunting and flexing her biceps, then lowered her to the floor. 'Yes, that's lovely. Thank you, my dear.'

Helga gave Melody and Freddie a short sharp nod, then left the room.

'She doesn't say much but she's got a heart of gold, our Helga,' Clementine said. 'Ten-time Olympic weightlifter and a former circus strongwoman.'

'That makes sense,' said Freddie, still shaking his head at Helga's strength. He accepted a biscuit and stuffed it into his mouth, sending crumbs flying everywhere as he added, 'So what do you do at The Workshop, Mumma Rose?'

'Other than boss us around?' Slack joked.

He suddenly threw five paintbrushes and a small unopened paint tin at Mumma Rose. Her arms stretched out like tentacles to catch them with ease, then she juggled them, twirling and bouncing and spinning them above her head without skipping a beat. Even Allira clapped along.

'Are you seeing what I'm seeing?' Freddie murmured to Melody, who was gaping in amazement.

Slack stood with his hands on his hips. 'Yeah, yeah, but who's going to ask me what *I* do?'

Allira smirked. 'We're waiting for you to show us, silly.'

'Very well,' said Slack, climbing up the staircase. Halfway along, he hoisted himself onto the railing.

'Not you too!' Melody said, peeking through her fingers.

'He's too close to the ground to flip ...' Freddie said.

'Just ... wait ...' Slack muttered, biting his lip in concentration. He sprang into the air and wrapped his fingers around the bottom of a giant hoop that Melody hadn't even noticed hanging from the ceiling in the cluttered and colourful room. He huffed and puffed as he hoisted himself up, wriggling and writhing until he was balanced inside it.

Melody and Freddie clapped.

'Not yet,' he groaned. 'There's more.'

'Now who's showing off?' Allira remarked, shaking her head.

Slack swung on the hoop, building up enough momentum for it to fly across to the other side of the room. With a sudden shout of glee, Slack launched himself from the hoop and soared through the air too.

His fingers wrapped around a long brown rope dangling from the ceiling, which he used to pull himself up to a wooden platform in the highest corner of the room.

'Couldn't have just taken the stairs like a normal human being, could he?' muttered Allira.

'What's so good about normal?' Slack called out, before walking across a high wire that was strung across the room.

'Okay, okay, I think that's enough excitement for one afternoon,' Clementine said, chomping on a biscuit. She turned to Melody and Freddie. 'Let's go to the studio out back. I've got something else to show you.'

* * *

They followed Clementine into a dark and poky room with a low ceiling that was crammed with wooden desks, artworks, circus equipment and guitars.

'Just ask her if you're that interested,' whispered Freddie to Melody.

'I'm *not* that interested,' Melody murmured back.

'Yes, you are! You couldn't stop staring.'

Clementine grinned. 'Ask me what?'

Freddie nudged Melody but she didn't say anything.

'Fine,' he said. 'I'll ask. That big wall in the other room — why is it empty? It looks so plain.'

Clementine struck a match and lit a row of candles on top of a broken old piano, sending a warm glow through the room. 'That wall isn't plain. It's a reminder that there's always space for something magical to happen in the world.'

Freddie crossed his arms over his chest. 'It just looked like an ordinary wall to me.'

Clementine shrugged. 'To you it may be ordinary. To me it says we create something out of nothing every day. I look at that blank wall and think of the endless ways I could colour it in. Isn't that exciting? We can all make the ordinary extraordinary in some way.'

'I guess so,' Freddie said, and he wandered off to examine a wire sculpture in the far corner of the studio.

'Did you say … *extraordinary*?' Melody asked Clementine, her heart fluttering.

'Well, yeah. Just look around you. Everything in here was created by someone from The Workshop. They brought something into the world that wasn't here before. Don't you think that's extraordinary?' She cleared her throat. 'It's like you and your writing. You took those words out of your head and put them on the page. Now they exist in the world!'

'They weren't meant to though,' Melody said. 'They were just meant for me. You took them, remember?'

'Found them, as I recall it. Someone had thrown them away.'

Melody pursed her lips. 'It's a long story.'

'Well, anyway, that notebook is your own way of leaving a mark, don't you think?' Clementine stepped forward. 'Speaking of which … I think we could really make something magic together.'

'But I can't paint or draw.'

'Forget that. I'm talking about music. Lyrics, songs, melodies … Melody!' Clementine grinned, and held up a ukulele that was sitting on a pile of dusty old books.

'I definitely can't do music,' Melody said, remembering her disastrous classes with Mr Pizzicato. 'Forget my name. My teacher tried everything — vocal lessons, every instrument in the world.'

Clementine scoffed. 'You do have music in you! You just haven't found your thing yet. Although if you ask me, maybe you already have …' She walked over to a music stand and picked up a sauce-stained brown leather-bound notebook. 'Here. As promised.'

Melody's eyes lit up at the sight of her most treasured possession.

Clementine passed it to her. 'Thank you so much for lending it to me.'

'I didn't lend —' She stopped as she took in Clementine's warm, friendly expression. 'You're welcome.'

She clutched the notebook to her chest, already feeling like a missing piece of her was back in place. She turned to Freddie. 'Ah, okay, I got my notebook back ... so maybe we should go now?'

'Just a second,' Clementine said. 'I meant what I said, Melody. You write beautiful lyrics. You should see the crowds I've been pulling. People are connecting with your words. Last week I made more money in one afternoon than I did all last month. I even saw a grown man crying into his potato and gravy.'

Melody shrugged. 'That's because of your performances. Your music and voice bring the words to life.'

'No, Melody, your words speak to people.'

'They do?' Melody blushed, and glanced in Freddie's direction.

He was curled up in a velvet armchair and flipping through a book of guitar sheet music. When he caught her gaze, he grinned. 'Listen to her!'

'Tell me this, Melody,' Clementine continued. 'When you have the kind of important thought you don't want to disappear into the air like it never happened, where does it go? Do you say it out loud in the dark? Do you yell it to your friends at school? Do you tell your parents across the dinner table?'

Melody paused. 'No. None of that.'

'So what do you do?'

'I write it down in my notebook.'

'Exactly!' Clementine clapped her hands. 'And that's why your words connect with people. They're real. People relate to them. They get what you're saying. They get *you*. And more than that, they feel like you understand. In a world where everyone's trying to find their place, you make people feel like they belong. Do you have any idea how hard that is?' Clementine's wide eyes locked with Melody's. 'That's why I brought you here today. I want us to keep doing that — together. You write the lyrics, and I'll write the music. Here, let me show you ...'

She pulled the ukulele in close to her chest and, closing her eyes, sang more of Melody's words.

Waiting and hoping,
For someone to see,
The girl in the tower,
And what she could be.

But life just goes on,
And things stay the same,
So from a distance she watches,
Away from the game.

Yet one day she's certain,
That someone will see,
The girl in the tower,
And what she will be.

Melody had to admit that her words sounded beautiful and eerie with Clementine's music. And she couldn't help noticing Freddie swaying along.

But none of this changed the fact that she didn't have the first clue about writing songs. All she knew was she had to get the words out of her head and into her notebook to feel normal. Otherwise she feared she might self-combust.

'I'm not sure, Clementine. That sounded good, but I don't think I'm the right person for this.'

'But you're already doing it,' Clementine said, 'and you're not even trying. The truth is … I'm all out of lyrics. I need more! My audience wants more original songs. We can be a team.'

Melody swallowed. She'd never been part of a team before.

'So how about it, Melody?' Clementine smiled. 'Are we going to make music together or what?'

16.

The magic begins

'Anything flowing yet, Melody?' Mumma Rose asked as she entered the studio with a jug fizzing with lemonade and a stack of colourful cups. 'This should keep everyone's creativity popping and crackling!'

Melody looked up from her notebook. She'd been staring at a blank page for ten minutes. 'I'm trying to write, but the words seem to have disappeared. I think I've scared them away.'

'They'll come back,' Mumma Rose said, handing Melody a cup. 'They're just taking a break, I'm sure.'

Freddie, squeezed next to Melody on an old velvet couch, was admiring the ceiling and its elaborate mural painted in every colour imaginable. 'I've got a word for you,' he said, clicking his fingers. 'Codswallop. Wackadoodle. Crackerjack, bombastic, gizmo!'

'Righto, Mr Dictionary,' Clementine said. 'Look out, world, we've got the creative dream team right here.'

Moe barked at this suggestion, causing Clementine to smile. 'Don't worry, Moe, you're part of the team, too. Geez, suddenly the prospect of not being in the spotlight goes to the fluffy little guy's head, doesn't it?' she teased, brushing her hand through his fur. Moe growled with pleasure, rolling on to his back to bare his stomach.

'These things can take time, Melody — much longer than you think,' Mumma Rose said with a reassuring smile. 'Keep trying. Clementine has shown me your scribblings and you're onto something special.'

A flush of embarrassment stained Melody's cheeks. She hadn't had this much attention for a long time. Well, positive attention. It was quite different from Mr Pizzicato's sighs whenever she played something on one of the instruments in his studio. She could almost hear his voice ringing in her ears: *I thought I'd heard everything that could go wrong by now, my dear Melody, but this … this is obscene! Let's try again from the top.*

She bit her lip, shuddering as she remembered Mr Pizzicato's abrupt disappearance. Thanks to Clementine and The Workshop, she'd almost forgotten about the Debut Gala but now it was all she could think about again. No wonder the words had abandoned her.

'Something on your mind?' Clementine asked, snapping Melody back into the real world.

'Um … have you heard of the Battyville Elite School For Musically Gifted Children's Debut Gala?'

'Sheesh, you rich folks love a fancy name, don't you? That sounds like the sort of event where Moe and I would get kicked out for breathing the same air as you lot.'

Moe gave a haughty bark.

'Just kidding, little bud, we know you're a dapper gent.' Clementine smirked. 'So, tell me more about this Gala.'

'It's a really important music recital — and the Prince and Princess of Zanjia are coming to watch.'

'I've seen them on the telly!' Clementine exclaimed. 'I watch the one in the window at Battyville Electrical sometimes. A real-life Prince and Princess — that's amazing. I heard the Princess can speak seven languages.'

'It's true,' Melody said. 'And it's not amazing, it's terrifying! They're coming to watch *me* — and like I've told you, I'm not musical, remember? My lack of talent has been a family secret for ten years, but once I get up on stage, it won't be a secret for much longer! My parents will never forgive me for destroying the Trumpet reputation.'

'Maybe you can't conduct orchestras like your father, but you've got something different,' said Clementine.

Mumma Rose nodded. 'Everyone has creativity inside them somewhere.'

'Not me. My music teacher, Mr Pizzicato, gave up on me after years of trying. He's mid-breakdown right now, probably drooling on a beach chair somewhere. I'm ordinary. And there's nothing my parents despise more than ordinary.'

'No one on this planet is ordinary,' Clementine scoffed. 'Everyone has something that makes them extraordinary. It just takes some people longer to find out what their something is.'

Melody sighed. 'That was a good speech, but this performance is going to be a disaster. I can't play the violin, the cello, the piano, the drums, the flugelhorn —'

'Whoa! Now you're just making up instruments!' Clementine said. 'Fine, so you're not going to be a world-famous *flugelhorn* player. But maybe you could sing? Surely with your mother's genes ...?'

Melody cleared her throat and launched into a shaky rendition of one of her songs, her voice crackling. *'Just once I'd like to be, in the kind of place that's in my head, the perfect place for me ...'*

Clementine scratched her chin, failing to hide her horror. 'Are you sure the flugelhorn isn't out of the question?'

Melody hung her head. 'It's hopeless.'

Clementine's finger found Melody's chin and gently lifted up her head. 'Not even close to hopeless. You know why? You're not alone any more. We'll find a way through this together, okay?'

'Clementine's right,' Mumma Rose said. 'You're part of The Workshop now. And when we work as a team, anything is possible. Now get back to that blank page. This poem isn't going to write itself.'

Melody curled up on the couch with her notebook, doodling in the top corner of the page. She thought about everything that had happened since Mr Pizzicato had abandoned her.

Meeting Freddie and sharing her secrets.

Visiting Town Square for the first time.

Riding through Battyville on the tandem bicycle with Clementine and Moe.

Discovering the magic of The Workshop.

And then suddenly the words came to her. First, a trickle or two; a sentence here, a verse there. And then a gushing flow of words that didn't stop.

As she wrote and rewrote, cutting out lines and shifting words around, she lost track of time and place. Nothing else mattered in the moment. All she could see were her pen scratchings in the notebook. All she could hear were the sentences dancing in her mind.

Before she knew it, she had scribbled down the first

draft of a poem. It was messy, it wasn't perfect, but it was the start of something. The blank page was no longer empty. It held possibilities.

Clementine cheered when Melody read the words out loud. 'A new song already! I can't wait to come up with some music and perform it soon.'

'Really?' Melody murmured.

'*Really.* You'll have to come with me to Town Square to see it in action. You too, Freddie. But now I'd better get you back to school before the Trumpets send out a search party.'

Clementine took Melody and Freddie back through the main room so they could say goodbye to everyone. Slack was doing a jig on the high wire; Allira was practising headstands on the staircase; Gaff was striding around on two-metre-tall stilts; and Mumma Rose was juggling twelve golf balls while hopping on one leg.

'Have we run away and joined the circus?' whispered Freddie.

Flushed with excitement, Melody clutched her notebook to her chest. 'Maybe.'

She wasn't quite sure what they had done, but she wanted to keep feeling this way.

17.

One extraordinary day

The crowd cheered as Melody and Clementine gave another bow. Freddie tipped his hat, then settled back down at his keyboard.

'See,' said Clementine to Melody, 'that wasn't so bad, was it?'

Melody looked at the audience's faces from under her baseball cap. They were all beaming from one ear to the other. She hadn't dared to sing, not even back-up vocals with Freddie, but she had faced her fear of public speaking and introduced the song. Clementine had told her it would be good practice to break down her fear of performing at the Debut Gala.

Clementine was so excited, she called out to the crowd, 'Keyboard by Freddie Bloom, vocals by me, and songwriting by the great and wonderful Mel—'

'Melanie,' Melody said before Clementine accidentally outed her. 'She always forgets my name. Too many lyrics and guitar chords rattling around in her head.'

'It's true,' Clementine said, before mouthing *sorry* to Melody. 'Luckily *Melanie* is here to set things straight.'

'Play another!' an old man yelled, waving his walking cane in the air. 'I've got gold coins to give away, but not for nothing!'

Clementine raised an eyebrow and Moe barked three times. 'Gold coins, you say, sir?' She settled down with her guitar, and gave Freddie the nod. 'Melo— ah, Melanie, maybe you can do the introduction for us again?'

She held up Melody's notebook turned to the page that Melody had been scribbling on at The Workshop. *The new poem.*

'Here?' Melody asked, blushing.

It was still hard to believe that Clementine and Freddie knew her poems so well. Poems that she had never dared to show anyone before. Well, she'd tried to show her parents a long time ago, but they'd always been too busy. *In a moment, child. I'm just sending the King and Queen of Lavenia one hundred and forty ostriches for an anniversary present*, Mr Trumpet had said. *Right after I'm done here*, Mrs Trumpet had said as she posed with a bejewelled crown on her head for yet another portrait to hang in the manor.

'Yes, here,' Clementine said. 'It's what the audience wants. And this is a good place to test out some new material.'

'But you haven't practised this one. I don't even know if the words work with music.'

'Then we'll make it work,' assured Freddie, fake-grinning at the waiting audience who were now shuffling and whispering among themselves.

'What if everyone laughs at us?' Melody asked.

Clementine smiled. 'Then we'll keep going with their laughter ringing in our ears.'

Melody couldn't believe it. Clementine made her feel like she could do anything — and it didn't matter if she didn't do it perfectly.

'Okay … let's do it,' she said.

'That's the spirit,' Clementine said. 'Remember, you're part of The Workshop now. We're a family and we work together.'

Freddie cracked his knuckles. 'What are you thinking for this one, Clementine? F minor?'

'Love it,' Clementine said.

Melody blinked. She still didn't really understand what F minor meant, even after years of Mr Pizzicato trying to teach her chords and scales. Somehow, they'd never stuck in her mind.

'Quick, Melody, say a little something before the gold coins roll in,' Clementine urged. 'Because they *will* roll in. And, Freddie, when she's finished, kick things off!'

Melody turned towards the crowd, which had squashed in closer around them.

'Hello, everyone,' she croaked. 'I'm Mel … Melanie.' She cleared her throat, then stood a little straighter and tilted her chin higher. 'This is a new poem … ah … song about how one day can change everything. And how even on that day you may not realise it's a special one-in-a-million moment. I hope you like it.'

Moe barked, signalling they had stalled for long enough. It was time to play Melody's brand new song.

Clementine and Freddie nodded at each other and began.

Here we are,
Just us four,
Hours in the sun,
Together on this day.

How long I have dreamed,
For a place such as this,
Where time disappears,
And adventure can begin.

It was all messy and new,
They smiled so I smiled too,
Everything to gain,
And nothing to prove,
On this day.

Clementine's voice quivered over the final line, and Freddie finished off the song with a note from his guitar that hung in the air.

They bowed in unison, and there was complete silence.

Melody's face felt hot with the embarrassment of everyone seeing straight into her heart. She wondered whether she should hurl herself face first into the water fountain in the middle of Town Square.

More silence — and then the crowd erupted, cheering and wrapping their arms around each other. The old man with the cane sobbed with happiness. Two little girls linked arms and danced in a circle, singing the song over and over in their sweet, squeaky voices.

Gold and silver coins rained into Clementine's guitar case. *Thump, shring, clink!* There were too many to count.

'You did this, Melody,' said Clementine. 'This is all because of you.'

'Because of *us*,' Melody insisted.

'Without your words, there'd be no music.'

'Without your music, no one would hear the words.'

Clementine grinned. 'Officially partners then.'

'Oi, where do I fit in?' asked Freddie.

Clementine smirked. 'You fit in just fine. Consider it the triangle of happiness.'

Moe barked, and licked Clementine's hand once, twice, a third time in case she missed it.

'We haven't forgotten you, fluffy one,' she told him, rolling her eyes. '*Rectangle* of happiness.'

'Or rhombus,' offered Freddie.

Melody smiled. 'A square of happiness.'

'It certainly is!' Clementine said, punching the air as coins and notes fell into the guitar case, some jumping over the sides onto the pavement.

Forget Trumpet Manor, the lavish pool, her four-poster bed — Melody didn't think she'd ever seen a sight so lovely as all those people caring about and connecting to their music.

As the last person drifted away singing a mish-mashed version of their songs, Clementine, Melody and Freddie hugged each other with excitement. Moe barked and ran around them in circles. Melody high-fived the others, even Moe. In that moment, she felt invincible.

Clementine tipped coins and notes into Melody's and Freddie's palms. 'We all earned this, so we all split it. Fair's fair.'

Melody stared at the coins. 'But I don't need the money. Freddie, tell her. You both need it more than I do.'

He shrugged. 'Leave me out of it.'

'But why?' Clementine asked her. 'You earned it. You should take your share.'

Melody thought of how grand Trumpet Manor was compared to the small terrace house where Clementine and the others lived, and Freddie's humble family home where he shared a bedroom with his brother and sister.

'I don't deserve it,' she said.

'Of course you do,' Clementine said, forcing more coins into Melody's hand. 'None of this would have happened without you.'

Melody shook her head and emptied the coins back into the guitar case. 'You know who I am,' she whispered. 'I have so much.' She crossed her arms, refusing to budge.

Freddie laughed. 'She does have a wing all to herself.'

Clementine raised an eyebrow. 'Fine. I can see we're not getting anywhere today.' She held up one shiny gold coin. 'Take this. Frame it, save it, spend it — whatever you want. Just please take it as a memory of today.'

Melody held out her palm. 'Okay, just that one. Thank you.'

Freddie elbowed her. 'When do we get to see inside that wing of yours?'

'One day,' Melody said, hope tingeing her voice. 'Hopefully one day soon.'

Smiling, she slipped the coin into her jacket pocket.

18.

Silly Mr Trumpet

Freddie threw a football high in the air and ran backwards towards the garden hedge with his arms and hands braced in position. He caught the ball with a grunt and said, 'We've got all weekend till we see Clementine again. She's got her tricks, and I've got mine. I'm sure I can teach you how to kick in that time.'

Whack! His foot connected with the ball, sending it flying towards Melody. She focused on it whizzing towards her, stretched her arms out and hoped for the best.

Thump! The ball made contact. She'd caught it first go.

'Not bad,' Freddie said.

Melody kicked the ball, sending it soaring high and far. It sailed over the hedge, over Trumpet Manor's high-security fence and out into the street.

Freddie's jaw dropped.

She flexed her muscles as a joke. 'Beginner's luck!'

'Well done, well done,' Freddie said, as they plopped down onto a soft patch of grass by the maze. 'So what's the plan for Monday? Town Square at lunchtime again? Shall we play another new song?'

Melody nodded. 'I'm working on something.'

She reached into her backpack and pulled out her notebook, then neatly tore out the page with her most recent poem scribbled on it. She slipped it into his hand. 'Here, take this. You can learn it before Monday.'

'Cool,' Freddie said, scanning the page.

Someone cleared their throat behind them. Melody's heart raced. They turned to see Mr Trumpet standing there, his thick arms folded over his chest.

'What's going on here, child?' he asked Melody, completely ignoring Freddie's presence even though his father had looked after the manor gardens for fifteen years.

Any children belonging to the Trumpets' staff were supposed to be rarely seen and never heard. Panicking, Freddie faked a cough and slipped the piece of paper covered in Melody's words into his mouth. Melody's jaw dropped in shock.

'Answer me, child! You should be in your wing, not out here,' Mr Trumpet added, twanging his suspenders in frustration.

'Sorry, Father,' Melody said. 'I … I … he … he was just looking for his ball. I think it went over the fence.'

Freddie shot Mr Trumpet an apologetic, closed-mouth smile.

'Very well, but he knows he shouldn't be in the gardens unsupervised. On your way, boy,' Mr Trumpet said. 'We've no time for games and silliness here. Melody needs to focus on her brilliant performance for the Debut Gala.'

Freddie nodded, gave an awkward bow and ambled off in the opposite direction. But as soon as Mr Trumpet's back was turned, he stuck his tongue out at Melody, revealing the page of words in his mouth. Melody breathed a sigh of relief when she saw that Freddie hadn't swallowed her only copy of the new song.

'Inside now, child,' Mr Trumpet scolded Melody as he shooed Freddie on his way. 'We can't have you out here cavorting with the staff. Oh, and before I forget: your mother wanted me to ask you how your practice is going? More improvements, I assume?'

Melody grimaced at the thought of Mr Pizzicato's abandoned studio. 'Actually,' she said, 'it's been a weird few days —'

'Splendid! Wonderful! Fantastic! I knew he'd be full of praise,' Mr Trumpet exclaimed as he looked at his watch.

'No, *a weird few days*. Father, I have to tell you something.' Melody sucked in a breath, preparing to confess that Mr Pizzicato had disappeared.

Mr Trumpet raised an eyebrow. 'For heaven's sake, Melody, I'm meeting your mother at an alumni soiree soon. I don't have time to stand around and gasbag with you.'

'Please. Let me say one thing. It's important.'

Mr Trumpet squatted down so they were eye to eye. 'Look, I'll tell you what's important. Your mother and I haven't always done everything right — we know that — but we've just wanted what was best for us. I mean, for you. The Debut Gala is just around the corner, and the Prince and Princess of Zanjia are so thrilled to be meeting you. Giving them the performance of a lifetime has to be your first priority,' he continued. 'It's time for you to take centre stage after all these years.'

'Mr Pizzicato is missing!' Melody blurted out. 'He's gone on holiday somewhere. I have no idea where, but I'm guessing the beach.'

Mr Trumpet raised an eyebrow, then erupted into high-pitched giggles. 'Mr Pizzicato on holiday? That's a good one, Melody. Now, we've chit-chatted enough and I'd better rush. Your mother will have Miss Sprinkles cook me up for dinner if I'm late again.' He patted her on the head, before trundling off still laughing. 'Next thing you'll be telling me you *still* can't sing. What a hoot!'

'I still can't sing,' Melody called after him.

His laughter became even louder. 'Well done, my girl, you're quite the joker. *Still can't sing.* Oh, it's good to laugh.'

His phone burst to life and he stopped to answer it. 'The Prince and Princess,' he mouthed to Melody and gave her a thumbs-up. 'Hello there, dear friends,' he boomed into the phone. 'We are so looking forward to welcoming you to Battyville. Melody was just telling me she can't wait to perform for you … Yes, her debut promises to be a most dazzling performance … Yes, yes, I quite agree. It will absolutely be something that people will talk about for years to come.'

Melody cringed as Mr Trumpet left the garden, still talking.

Her father wasn't wrong. If she was forced to go through with the Debut Gala, people would definitely be talking about her performance for years to come.

19.

A visit from Principal Sharp

Melody and her parents relaxed in the sunshine by their outdoor pool. It was twice the size of an Olympic pool, shaped like a musical note, surrounded by lush palm trees and heated to the perfect temperature all year round. Melody had only ever paddled in the pool on her own before, but today her mother had invited her to join her and her father for a late-afternoon swim. It was a reward for Melody's hard work with Mr Pizzicato in the lead-up to the Debut Gala.

After her failed attempt to tell Mr Trumpet the truth, Melody hadn't tried again. It was too nice to spend time together as a family — she didn't want to spoil it.

Mrs and Mr Trumpet lay on sun lounges in matching leopard-print robes, while Melody splashed in the water on a giant inflatable guitar, sipping lemonade from a coconut and listening to the birds chirping in the trees above. There was no tutoring, no expectations, no pressure. It was all she had ever wanted.

As she gulped down another fizzy mouthful, Melody spotted Miss Sprinkles hurrying towards the pool.

'Excuse me, Mrs Trumpet, Mr Trumpet ... you have ... a visitor,' Miss Sprinkles said, struggling to catch her breath. 'Principal Sharp is here!'

'Cripes with cream!' Mrs Trumpet said, tightening her robe. 'What does she want?'

'Principal Sharp is *here*? At the manor?' asked Melody. 'Like ... right now?'

'Yes,' Miss Sprinkles said. 'She was most insistent that she talks to you. Apparently it's about the Debut Gala.'

'Oh,' Melody said, taking another big gulp of lemonade. That didn't sound good. It didn't sound good at all.

'Ma'am, Royce is with Principal Sharp in the foyer now, awaiting your orders,' Miss Sprinkles said. 'What should I tell him?'

'I don't understand this woman,' said Mrs Trumpet. 'Everything is perfectly under control. Mr Pizzicato is making progress with the child, and Melody has her gown from Claudette Rouge. Her debut performance

144

is going to be a spectacular success.' She turned to Mr Trumpet. 'What do you think could be so important, my sweet cherry plum?'

'What was that, darling?' Mr Trumpet asked. He was preoccupied with struggling to roll around to face them all.

'Allegra Sharp,' huffed Mrs Trumpet. 'She's here. She's obsessed with us.'

'Who wouldn't be obsessed with you, my love?' Mr Trumpet cooed. 'The woman is only human.'

Mrs Trumpet sighed and fluffed her hair. 'It is a blessing and a curse. But hasn't she heard of a little thing called privacy? Oh, bring her here, Miss Sprinkles. Let's get this over with.'

'I'll let Royce know, ma'am,' Miss Sprinkles said, and bowed before scurrying back to the manor.

Melody sucked in a breath, suddenly feeling cornered. She took in the complicated garden maze to her left, the larger-than-life-sized gold statues of her parents by the pool, the high-security fence to her right. There was no escape. She was trapped.

Principal Sharp greeted them all with a tight smile.

'Hello, Allegra, welcome to our humble home,' said Mrs Trumpet, clicking into the gushing mode she usually saved for the grey-haired members of the Opera Board during awards season. 'I was just saying to Barry that we haven't seen you in what feels like forever. You've been missed.'

'That's far too kind of you,' Principal Sharp said. 'I won't stay long though.'

'What a shame,' Mrs Trumpet lied. 'Anyway, how can we be of help?'

'As you know, we're days away from the Debut Gala so I'm doing the rounds of every child's family to make sure things are on track,' Principal Sharp said. 'It can be a nerve-racking time for our brilliant students and their parents.'

'Nerves? From a Trumpet? Never!' chimed in Mr Trumpet. 'In fact, Melody is exceeding expectations.'

Mrs Trumpet jutted out her chin. 'The Prince and Princess of Zanjia will be positively dazzled, we assure you. It's shaping up to be an event to remember.'

'Wonderful,' Principal Sharp said. 'I'd expect nothing less from the Trumpet heir. What an honour for us to finally experience her prodigious talent in person. And to think she's achieved it all without Mr —'

'Yes, yes, the child is wonderful, she can't stop achieving, you're all up-to-date,' said Mrs Trumpet, gently leading Principal Sharp back towards the manor. 'If we're all done here …?'

Melody thought she was safe — until Principal Sharp added, 'I must say, Viola, between you and me

I'm relieved Melody is still shining. I wasn't sure *what* to expect when Mr Pizzicato went on holiday so suddenly.'

Mrs Trumpet stopped abruptly and her eyebrows shot up in shock. But she quickly recovered and forced another fake smile. 'Mmm,' she murmured, glaring at Melody.

Melody felt her cheeks flush red. She sucked in another long gulp of lemonade.

'But of course you've managed to secure another wonderful music tutor, just as he suggested,' continued Principal Sharp. 'What a fool I was for doubting the great talent of the Trumpet heir without Mr Pizzicato by her side. Of course she's thriving. Please, forgive my ignorance, Viola, but I'm sure you understand his departure came as quite the surprise after all these years.'

'Ahhh, yes, it was a little surprising,' Mrs Trumpet said with a thin smile. 'A little surprising indeed.'

* * *

'You could not *be* in more trouble, child!' bellowed Mrs Trumpet as she paced up and down the side of the pool.

Melody cowered in the water behind her coconut. 'But Mother —'

'But Mother nothing!' Mrs Trumpet raged. 'Oh, Barry, can you believe this disaster? The lies! So many lies!'

'Lies, yes, awful,' he said, fishing a chocolate doughnut out of his robe pocket and chomping into the icing. 'Wait … what lies again, turtle dove?'

Mrs Trumpet groaned but kept her glaring gaze on Melody. 'She's been lying to all of us. Me. You, my sweet. Royce. Spending time at school with no supervision, doing heaven knows what. It's a wonder that she hasn't landed us on the front page of the newspaper! "Battyville Girl Reaches New Levels of Stupidity By Lying to Loving, Supportive Parents". And to think Mr Pizzicato has gone off and left us to deal with this mess on our own.'

'He has?' Mr Trumpet shook his fist in the air. 'Outrageous!'

'Keep up, Barry,' huffed Mrs Trumpet. She teetered back and forth along the side of the pool, her heels clicking on the tiles, a stomping, fuming tower of anger. Melody was surprised there weren't flames scorching from her mother's mouth.

'But … but … things *have* been progressing, haven't they, child?' Mr Trumpet asked Melody. 'The Debut Gala is so soon, and the public is eagerly anticipating your performance. Not to mention their Royal Highnesses!'

Melody gulped. Sometimes you have to be brave, she thought. You have to do the thing you don't want to do. Tell the truth, even if your heart's thumping so fast you think it might burst straight through your chest.

'I'm not really progressing. In fact the whole thing is going to be a disaster because Mr Pizzicato has left and I can't sing and I can't play an instrument and I have no idea what I'm doing,' Melody said in one long breath.

'Enunciate, my child,' Mr Trumpet said, leaning closer.

Mrs Trumpet let out a gurgled shriek. 'For goodness sake, Barry, the little clam is just confirming what we already knew. She's hopeless, Mr Pizzicato has gone and the Debut Gala performance is doomed.'

'There has to be a mistake,' Mr Trumpet said. 'There has to be. All that time, all that money … she has to have improved.'

Melody knew there was no clearer way to say it. So she didn't. Instead, she swam to the edge of the pool, pulled herself out of the water and sang.

'*Here we are, just us four, hours in the sun, together on this day,*' she squeaked and crackled. '*How long I have dreamed, for a place such as this …*'

By now her parents were kneeling on the tiles with their heads in their hands.

'Enough!' Mr Trumpet cried, holding up his hand in surrender. 'I can't take it any more. What shall we do, my darling Viola?'

'It's time for Plan B,' Mrs Trumpet said without missing a beat. 'The Prince and Princess will be arriving in Battyville any minute. If they, or the media, get a sniff of something peculiar, everything will be ruined.'

'Plan B?' asked Melody, her teeth chattering as she reached for her towel. 'What do you mean?'

'Just remember, this is all your doing,' Mrs Trumpet hissed at her. 'You drove Mr Pizzicato away! He was our last hope.'

'But I tried my best,' Melody protested. 'That's all I can do. He shouldn't have left me.'

'ENOUGH!' Mr Trumpet roared.

'You're right, my scrumptious one,' Mrs Trumpet said. 'The time has come. My child, we can't have you here any more.'

Tears stung Melody's eyes. 'But this is my home.'

'We'll send you to a new home,' Mr Trumpet said. 'A wonderful boarding school overseas: Dullard Private. It's far, far away from Battyville and the Debut Gala.'

'Please don't do this!' Melody pleaded. 'I won't know a soul.'

Mrs Trumpet sighed. 'That's the point, our dear little ferret. You'll have a fancy new name and a fancy new look. No one will know you. Think of it as a fresh start.'

'A chance to be a better you,' Mr Trumpet added. 'The person you could have been if you weren't born into this life with us.'

Melody cocked her head to one side. 'So you don't want to be my parents any more?'

'We'll still be your parents. We'll just be on the other side of the world,' Mr Trumpet said.

'How long will I have to be away?' Melody asked.

His jaw hardened. 'Just until all this drama dies down. Until the pressure is off.'

'But that could take years.' Melody's throat felt tight. 'What if we just tell everyone the truth now? No more lies. We'll finally be free.'

Mr Trumpet sighed. 'You just don't get it.'

'Royce!' Mrs Trumpet screeched. 'Royce!'

Royce hurried over from standing guard by the nearby bushes. 'Yes, ma'am?' he asked, chest puffed out.

'Take the child to her room. Lock the door and guard the hallway.'

'Yes, ma'am,' Royce said.

'No ...' Melody's mind raced with everything she would leave behind: Clementine and her music; Freddie, her first ever friend; and Moe with his grumpy little face and muddy paws. 'Please, don't do this,' she begged.

'And, Royce,' Mrs Trumpet continued, 'confiscate any computers or phones or ... or *notebooks* that you can find hidden in her room. Anything she could use to get a message out.'

'Mother, no!' Melody said. 'You can't send me away. Please, I beg you. You haven't even let me say goodbye to anyone!'

'Who on earth could you possibly have to say goodbye to?' Mrs Trumpet asked.

'Get it done,' Mr Trumpet ordered Royce.

He nodded and turned in Melody's direction. Jaw clenching, Melody sprinted past him along the wet tiles.

'Stop her, Royce!' Mrs Trumpet cried, tottering towards them in her heels. 'I said, stop her!'

Royce lurched at Melody, who shrieked and ducked out of the way.

'Grab her!' Mrs Trumpet ordered as Melody hurried along the tiles, slipping and sliding in her attempt to escape. 'Quickly, before she — oof!'

Melody had crashed into her mother, sending them both into the pool with a huge *SPLASH!* Water sprayed everywhere, drenching Mr Trumpet and Royce. Mrs Trumpet burst up to the surface, mascara running down her cheeks.

'Royce!' she gurgled, as Melody appeared beside

her, also spluttering water. 'Seize the child and take her upstairs immediately.'

'Yes, ma'am,' Royce said, wringing out his shirt and jacket.

'Out you come, my poor little possum,' Mr Trumpet said as he pulled Mrs Trumpet from the pool. Her once-perfect curled hair was dripping and flopped over her forehead. One heel was missing.

Mrs Trumpet grunted. 'Remember, Royce, she's to have no contact with anyone,' she told him. 'The child will be on her way to Dullard Private by the end of the week.'

The end of the week. It was all over.

As a soaking Melody shuffled up the staircase to her bedroom, Royce thudding behind her, she wondered if she would ever walk through this house again. If her parents were banishing her because she couldn't sing or play an instrument, why would they ever bring her home?

Melody was never going to be a performer like them. She would never be enough.

20.

The Trumpets' wicked plan

'Breaking news out of Battyville,' said the newsreader on the television. 'The heir of the Trumpet empire, ten-year-old Melody Trumpet, has been kidnapped.'

Melody, who was very much *not* kidnapped but locked in her private wing with Royce guarding her, shook her head and bashed on the door again.

'I haven't been kidnapped! I'm right here!' she yelled. 'Help! Someone! Save me!'

'According to sources,' the newsreader continued, 'the only child of the musical icons — a prodigy who was due to give her debut performance in front of the Prince and Princess of Zanjia — was reported missing after failing to show up for dinner last night. Viola and Barry T Trumpet are working with authorities to try to bring Battyville's golden girl home.

'Crossing now to our reporter on the ground just outside Trumpet Manor. Are there any updates on little Melody's whereabouts?'

'Thank you, Christine,' the reporter said. 'None of the reported sightings hold up at this stage. However, if anyone has any information they're urged to contact police as soon as possible. The clock is ticking.'

'Have you spoken to the Trumpets?'

'I have, and they are devastated. Viola Trumpet is so heartbroken she broke down on camera, wailing in pitch-perfect key.'

'Tragic indeed. Such an extraordinary family. How could this terrible thing happen to them only days before the prestigious Debut Gala?'

'It's a question we're all asking, and hopefully we'll have some answers soon. For now, let's hope young Melody is safe and unharmed.'

'Hope is all we have. And yes, here's to her safe return.'

Melody switched off the television in a huff.

She went to her window, which was slightly ajar, and tried once again to slide it open. It wouldn't budge. Grimacing, Melody gave it another tug. Her arm muscles quivered and ached but she wasn't strong enough to open it. The window was stuck, just like her.

Melody's gaze fell on a large yellow umbrella hanging from a hook behind her door. She took the brolly and aimed its pointy tip at the open window. The umbrella trembled as Melody tried to lever the window open, but then ... *SNAP!* The brolly collapsed under the strain.

Melody drew in a deep breath.

She looked outside past the enormous tree winding its way past her window and into the sky, and gazed down into the manor gardens. Freddie was sitting on the grass, playing his guitar and chatting to Mr Bloom who was pruning a hedge. There it was. A ray of hope. A small chance at freedom. Melody called out to Freddie for help through the sliver in the window but her words got lost in the wind. She tried again, screaming until her throat burned, but she was too high, too far away.

Melody wondered if Freddie believed she'd been kidnapped. Surely not? But then again ... why wouldn't he? She wasn't going to be peeking at him through the window of the secret passage, and she wouldn't show up at Town Square either.

Freddie may know her parents were eccentric, but he had no idea they could go so far as to fake a kidnapping to save their reputation. Melody wouldn't have believed it herself if Royce hadn't been guarding her bedroom door all night.

The bedroom door rattled, causing her to jump.

It was just Royce, struggling to balance the key and a silver tea tray covered with fluffy white scones, a jug of cream and a bowl of blood-red jam.

'Mealtime, Miss Trumpet,' he said, and lumbered towards Melody's desk to put down the tray.

Melody took two scones. If she was going to be sent away, she may as well have a stomach full of Miss Sprinkles' delicious scones, jam and cream.

Royce hummed to himself as he placed the spoons into the bowls of jam and cream. The ditty sounded familiar. Out of tune, but familiar.

'What's that song?' Melody asked him.

He paused. 'You know, I'm not sure, but it's catchy. You were humming it yesterday — something about "together on this day" — and it's been stuck in my head ever since.'

It was her song. Melody's heart panged at the thought of never seeing Clementine, Freddie, Moe or The Workshop troupe again.

While Royce was distracted with the tea, Melody peeked outside and saw that Freddie had swapped his guitar for a shovel. But he wasn't using it. He was still daydreaming, probably imagining the crowd cheering and throwing gold coins the next time the three of them performed in Town Square.

157

Melody clenched her fists. If only she could contact her friend to tell him what was happening. Or maybe she could …

'Royce,' she said, crossing her legs and hopping from side to side. 'I really need to … you know.'

He cocked his head in confusion. 'Dance?'

'No.'

'Skip?'

'No!'

'What is it, Miss Trumpet?' he asked, growing impatient.

'I need to … you know …!'

His eyes widened. 'Number one?'

Melody pursed her lips. 'Royce! I need to go. Now. And I need some privacy.'

He crinkled his nose. 'You've got one minute.'

'These things can't be rushed,' Melody said. 'I need to soap my hands, and rinse my hands, and dry my hands —'

'Four minutes,' he said. 'And not a second longer.'

* * *

Melody told herself to count to ten while she waited inside the bathroom, but only made it to six before impatience got the better of her. Holding her breath, she opened the bathroom door slowly to avoid it creaking or groaning and peeked out. Royce, his back to her, was pacing the hallway and humming to himself again.

Guarded toilet breaks, locking her in her bedroom, a fake kidnapping — these were new lows for her parents. Was fame *really* worth all this?

She snuck out of the bathroom, gently closing the door behind her, and tiptoed in the opposite direction from Royce, until she reached a door that led to another corridor. Melody opened it and sprinted along a hallway that wasn't as opulent as those in the main part of the manor. She was in the servants' quarters now and she knew exactly where she wanted to go. To the staff entrance.

She ran past doors and rooms, up steps, down steps, around corners, not daring to look left or right, focused only on making it to her destination. Breathless, she finally reached a thick brown door. She dragged it open to see a steep, twisting concrete staircase that she knew led out to the garden.

Melody pounded down the steps, and paused in the doorway that led to the gardens. She could see Mr Bloom and Freddie arguing over how to use a rake properly. She tried not to laugh as she watched Freddie rolling his eyes. He may have been top of his classes at school, but he hadn't inherited Mr Bloom's passion for gardening.

Melody couldn't risk being spotted by anyone other than Freddie, so she needed to get creative. She looked around for something — *anything* — to write on. Her gaze settled on a neat pile of leaves, bark and twigs under a nearby tree. She crept over, hid behind the thick, gnarly trunk, and squatted down to pluck a sharp stick from the pile.

She found a large piece of bark and scratched *SOS. MT not kidnapped. Locked in bedroom!* onto it. She knew it was a desperate move, but she was willing to try anything to avoid Dullard Private.

Please work, she thought, before tiptoeing towards Mr Bloom's gardening tools. Freddie's backpack was sitting next to them. *Jackpot!*

Freddie's argument with his father had turned into a leaf-throwing competition. Within moments, they were chasing each other around the garden with their rakes, before cracking up laughing and crash-tackling each other into a wrestling match on the grass.

Glad of the distraction, Melody unzipped the front of Freddie's backpack. Screwing up her nose at the sight of a soggy blueberry muffin squashed in there, she thrust the piece of bark inside, then just as quickly zipped the bag shut again.

She sprinted back through the staff door, up the staircase and along the winding hallway, until she reached the door to her own hallway. Royce was still pacing up and down and humming.

The moment his back was turned, Melody raced to her bathroom door. Then she gave the door a nudge, causing it to swing, and pretended she'd just stepped out.

'Four minutes,' she announced. 'As promised.'

Back in her bedroom, Melody rushed to the window. The Blooms were gone. So were Mr Bloom's tools and Freddie's backpack. She hoped Freddie found her message before it was too late.

All she had now was hope.

21.

Performance of a lifetime

'Is that everything you want to take?' Mrs Trumpet asked Melody. She sat her plump behind on the suitcase in an attempt to close it.

'What I want is to not go at all,' Melody said. 'I have friends in Battyville!'

'But they're forbidden.' Mrs Trumpet's eyes narrowed. 'Who are they?'

Melody didn't reply.

'Well, you won't be seeing them again anyway. You're leaving tomorrow so keep packing – and no more tantrums. We're not turning around the private jet if you forget anything.'

'I'm not going away forever.' Melody crossed her arms over her chest. 'Or am I?'

Mrs Trumpet bounced on her bottom to squash

the suitcase down a little more. 'Forever is such a strong word. So permanent. I prefer to think of this as an eternally temporary change. What you fail to understand, child, is that being a Trumpet isn't just a name. It's a lifestyle and, more importantly, a business. We must all protect the family reputation. Besides, I heard your new school has a swimming pool … isn't that great?'

'We have a pool here!' Melody said.

'Listen, you little ant, your father and I have spent decades building the Trumpet empire. And before that, it was years and years of music practice, no friends, no holidays, just doing what my mother told me to build my career. I refuse to have all my hard work destroyed because you've failed to live up to expectation. With you away at boarding school, we all benefit. You get a future, and your father and I get —'

'A life without me,' Melody interrupted, voice cracking.

'You'll get used to it eventually,' Mrs Trumpet said. She turned on the television with a swirl of the remote. 'Look, you're all packed so you can distract yourself for a while. *Relax*.'

A commercial featuring Clive the soprano chicken blared on the screen. Melody watched the chicken strutting, pecking and bobbing to the beat. She turned off the television. She didn't need any more reminders that she was the one person on Earth that Mr Pizzicato couldn't teach.

Mrs Trumpet checked her watch. 'Better run and touch up my make-up before dinner.' She noticed Melody's questioning expression. 'We're hosting some of the country's most senior journalists before the press conference about your, well ... *disappearance*. I can't have them seeing me like this. Appearances are everything.'

'You invited the media into our house?' Melody nearly choked at her parents' nerve.

'Problem?' asked Mrs Trumpet with wide eyes.

'You don't feel guilty about sending everyone on the most pointless search in history?'

'It takes immense sacrifice to get to the top,' her mother said. 'And sometimes you need to do all sorts of unsavoury things to stay there.' She paused, then burst into tears. 'Oh, our dear girl ... our dear Melody. What will we do without her? All these years spent watching her grow and thrive ... then poof! Gone. Snatched away in the night.'

Melody watched in shock as her mother dabbed away tears. Mascara smudged her cheeks and her eyelashes were thick and gooey. And her outlandish performance wasn't finished yet.

Mrs Trumpet honked into her dainty handkerchief. 'We were supposed to be celebrating her first ever public performance at the Battyville Elite School For Musically Gifted Children's Debut Gala tomorrow night, with the Prince and Princess of Zanjia. In the very hall where Barry T Trumpet and I met all those years ago. But instead, here we are, begging for any information at all about our daughter's whereabouts. If you know anything, please contact the police immediately.

'And instead of the Debut Gala, which we're sure you understand would be just too devastating in the tragic circumstances, we will be holding a charity event in Melody's honour at Crescendo Hall. Please do join us for that special occasion. And we apologise to all the other students who will miss out on making their debuts this year.'

Pause.

Mrs Trumpet broke into a wide grin and gave an exaggerated bow. 'And ... cut! What do you think? Did you believe me?'

'Yes,' Melody said. 'I even almost believed you'll miss me.'

Mrs Trumpet cocked her head to one side. 'Perfect. Although I'd better work on it before we go live to air. And change into a show-stopping outfit, of course.

People can be so cruel if you don't get everything just right.'

'They really can be,' Melody said, but subtlety wasn't Mrs Trumpet's strong point.

'We all have dreams,' her mother continued, 'but they don't always come true, no matter how much we might want them to.' She sighed, and reached out a hand to stroke Melody's cheek, not noticing when Melody pulled away. 'Rest up, and I'll see you in the morning. And wish me luck! This feels like the most important show of my life.'

With a flick of her feather boa, Mrs Trumpet hurried out the door.

* * *

Nibbling on her fingernails, Melody watched Mrs Trumpet on the television as she performed at the press conference. And perform she did. After all, she was on a stage in a magnificent gown, her yellow feather boa around her neck, and a camera in her face. She swooned, she gasped, she sobbed and she dabbed away tears with a delicate white handkerchief, just as she had practised, all while making sure her best side was facing the camera. Everyone loved Mrs Trumpet and she loved them right back — more than she loved just about anything else, maybe even Mr Trumpet. The journalists fussed and fought over who got to speak to her next, thrusting their microphones into her face. Mr Trumpet stood at her side, nodding along as Mrs Trumpet made a teary plea for Melody's immediate return.

Melody switched off the screen, her mother's words from earlier pulsating in her mind. Maybe she would be better off living far away from her family. Perhaps the new school could be the perfect place for her. She could be herself, write in her notebook anytime she pleased, and she wouldn't be scolded for not knowing how to sing opera in four languages by age three.

Then she plunged her hand into her pocket and her fingers wrapped around the gold coin Clementine had given her. Or maybe she'd already found her perfect place, and it was with her new friends. She could be herself at The Workshop too, and there was an entire blank wall there to remind her of life's amazing possibilities. Clementine, Freddie and the troupe at The Workshop could be her family — the kind of family that you weren't born into, but which you never let go of if you were lucky enough to find them.

She smiled as she imagined Moe's insulted bark at being left out. Clementine, Freddie *and Moe* could be her family, she corrected herself.

All of a sudden, her bedroom window rattled. Melody sat up and saw two bodies edge into view. It was Freddie and Clementine and they were standing on her windowsill!

22.

Breaking in

Melody's heart pounded as she took in the sight of their palms, noses and bodies pressed up against the glass. Clementine's eyebrows were raised into a panicked, clown-like 'I've made a huge mistake' expression, while Freddie's gaze darted between Melody, the dizzying drop and the mighty tree behind them. He looked tempted to leap back into its branches and never return. Melody didn't blame him. Her friends had endured a death-defying climb up the tree — and their position on the windowsill was just as precarious.

'It's stuck!' Melody shouted, exaggerating the words so Clementine and Freddie could lip-read through the thick glass. 'I can't open it!'

Freddie and Clementine swapped worried looks. Clementine snuck a glance down and Melody saw her swallow hard, then her focus returned to the window to see if there was an alternative way inside. Eyes clamped shut in terror, Freddie edged closer to Clementine, then his left foot slipped from the ledge.

Melody screamed and pressed her hands up against the glass. 'Freddie!'

Freddie flailed about for a few moments before finding his footing.

'Hold on!' Melody cried out.

'Grease!' Clementine yelled. 'Find something to grease the window!'

Freddie watched on, his skin turning a few shades paler from fear, as Melody sprinted around looking for something — *anything* — else that might help loosen the window's tracks.

'Hurry!' Freddie snuck another look at the huge drop below. 'Hurry, Melody!'

Brow furrowed, Melody opened her wardrobe and glared at the empty racks. She slammed the doors then ran to her vanity to rifle through the drawers, tossing empty boxes and trays left, right and centre. Her most precious possessions were already packed for Dullard Private — everything left behind had served its purpose. All that remained were her too-small clothes and shoes; her tutor's textbooks and academic notes;

and the used wax candles that lined the mantel of the old fireplace in the corner.

Melody paused.

The candles.

She snatched one from the mantel, raced to the window and rubbed the wax candle into the grooves of the glass window's track. Grimacing, she tried to drag the window open, but it was still stuck.

'Keep going!' Clementine yelled. 'You can do this, Melody!'

Freddie didn't say a word. His legs trembled as he clung to Clementine.

Melody continued to press the wax into the track, rubbing it back and forth until her arms burned. She gave it one last rub then pulled on the sliding window again. This time, it groaned open. Without wasting another second, Freddie and Clementine clambered through the window and collapsed into her bedroom.

'You're alive!' Clementine said. She gave an exhausted cheer.

'And so are we,' puffed Freddie. He threw himself onto Melody's bed, sneakers and all. 'Barely.'

'I can't believe you're here,' Melody said.

Clementine, who was flushed bright pink after the climb, grinned. 'And I can't believe you saved us!'

Melody smiled. 'So you found my SOS in your backpack?'

'Mmm-hmm,' Freddie said, still regaining his colour. 'That's what friends are for.'

'My arms are weaker than I realised,' groaned Clementine. 'I should have sent Allira, Slack and Gaff up here instead of having them boost us up the tree then leaving them on guard below. They would have done five somersaults and got into the building easily.'

'Listen — things are bad,' Melody said, glancing at her closed bedroom door. 'You're in danger just being here. My parents have cancelled the Debut Gala and they're sending me —'

'Wait, there's really no Gala?' Freddie asked.

Melody rolled her eyes. 'Pay attention! It gets worse.'

'Hellooooooooooooooo!' A high-pitched voice rang through the air and the door burst open. It was Mrs Trumpet, glowing with happiness after the media conference, with Mr Trumpet on her arm.

The Trumpets' jaws dropped at the sight of Melody on the floor, Freddie on the bed and Clementine sitting on the windowsill.

'What in the …?' stammered Mr Trumpet.

But Mrs Trumpet's brain had already gone into overdrive. 'Intruders!' she screamed, pointing at Freddie. 'Barry, there's an army of journalists drinking coffee downstairs! Grab the puny maggot before they spot him!'

A baffled Mr Trumpet lunged towards Freddie, who leaped off the bed and ran for the door. Mrs Trumpet stuck her high heel out, tripping Freddie. He crashed to the carpet. By the time he'd scrambled to his feet, Mr Trumpet had him by the arm.

'Now the girl!' shrieked Mrs Trumpet. 'The girl! Quick, before someone sees her!'

Melody jumped in front of Clementine. 'Mother, leave them alone. They're my friends.'

'*Friends*? Do they know your secret?'

Melody gritted her teeth, chin thrust upwards in defiance. She didn't reply.

Mrs Trumpet shrieked and stamped her foot. 'Barry, she must leave tonight! We can't have her on the premises a second longer — the secret is spreading. They know too much. They know it all. Call for the jet right now.'

'They know nothing!' Melody fibbed. 'Let them go.'

'I'm sorry, Melody,' Clementine whispered behind her. 'We tried.'

'Royce!' Mrs Trumpet shrieked into the hallway. 'Royce! Come at once!'

Royce rushed into the bedroom and tripped over Freddie and Mr Trumpet, who were now wrestling on the floor.

'Do something, Royce!' Mrs Trumpet screamed.

But he was all tangled up with Freddie and Mr Trumpet.

'Fools!' Mrs Trumpet smoothed down her dress and hair, and narrowed her eyebrows. 'I'll take care of this myself.'

She stormed towards Clementine, but Melody grabbed the feather boa wrapped around her mother's neck and yanked it with all her might. Feathers went flying everywhere.

'My boa!' Mrs Trumpet cried, kneeling down to gather up the loose feathers. 'The girl, Barry — seize the girl!'

'Yes, my darling,' he huffed, and trundled towards the window, leaving Freddie hooked under Royce's arm. But as he surged towards Clementine, he slipped on some feathers and fell flat on his back.

Clementine laughed at Mr Trumpet's impromptu backflip and didn't notice Mrs Trumpet moving towards her. Mrs Trumpet seized Clementine's arm and they struggled together on the windowsill.

'Be careful!' Melody cried out.

Clementine tried to free herself from Mrs Trumpet's grip, yanking her arm once, twice — but on her third try she pulled too hard and tumbled backwards, right out the window.

'Clementine!' Melody and Freddie shouted in unison.

The rosy colour drained from Mrs Trumpet's cheeks, leaving her ghostly pale. Her lips thinned into a hard line. 'Royce, take the boy downstairs,' she said. 'Melody, I'll deal with you soon.'

'But Clementine ...' Melody said, still in shock. 'Is she alright?'

Mrs Trumpet looped her now-featherless boa around her neck and repeated, 'I'll be back to deal with you soon.'

Melody's gaze locked with Freddie's. They didn't speak a word but their glistening eyes said everything.

Royce dragged Freddie out of the bedroom, and the Trumpets followed, locking the door behind them.

Melody hurried to the window and looked down, expecting to see her friend lying injured on the ground.

But there was no Clementine, just the manicured gardens of Trumpet Manor.

23.

Over the fence

'I'm alive, I'm alive, I'm alive,' puffed Clementine as she, Allira, Slack and Gaff sprinted through the gardens, their hearts pounding, their feet thumping on the grass. 'But everything is spinning … *am* I alive?'

'You are,' confirmed Gaff. A large net hung over his shoulder — the same net the troupe had used to catch Clementine when she tumbled from the window. 'Now move it! We didn't get that much of a head start.'

The foursome raced through the grounds, past the enormous music-note-shaped pool, the larger-than-life-sized gold statues of Mr and Mrs Trumpet, the garden maze, and a menagerie filled with exotic animals from all around the world.

'Are those llamas?' asked Allira, her eyes widening as she paused to let Clementine catch up. 'Come on, Clementine — hurry!'

'I'm … trying … to …' Clementine clutched her sides in pain. 'What about Freddie? And Melody? We should go back for them.'

'And risk getting captured too?' Gaff replied. 'We'll have to work out a new plan and come back. But we'll find them.'

Clementine rubbed at her stomach. 'I can't keep up. This stitch is killing me. Tell Moe I love him and go on without me.'

'Tempting, but no,' Allira said, grabbing Clementine's hand and dragging her along. 'You know Mumma Rose's spiel about sticking together!'

'How could we forget?' laughed Slack, jogging along with ease.

'Focus, you lot,' Gaff shouted back at them. 'There's a fence around this next corner so save your energy.'

Clementine puffed her way after the group. As she turned the corner, she gaped at the sight before them. The Trumpets' high-security fence towered into the sky. It was at least ten metres tall, and made of steel bars with sharp spikes and barbed wire on top.

'Okay, this is bad,' she said. 'This is really bad.'

The rest of the group rushed towards the fence. Allira got there first and threw herself at the bars, pulling herself up the metal.

'There's no time to lose,' she called down to the others. 'Climb!'

Clementine groaned. 'But I'm just a musician!'

'Slack, follow your sister up there,' Gaff ordered. 'And Clementine, hop on my back. I'll carry you over the fence.'

Slack clambered up with ease behind Allira, who was nearly at the top.

Biting her lip, Clementine wrapped her arms around Gaff's neck. 'Thanks,' she told him.

'Hang onto me! We're going up.'

He reached for the bars and, with an almighty groan, pulled himself and Clementine up the first metre.

'Don't look down,' Clementine murmured to herself, eyes clamped shut. 'Everything is going to be alright. Everything is going to be — *argh*!' Something had grabbed at her legs.

She looked down to see Royce swearing and straining as he clasped her by the ankles, struggling to pull her down. 'You trespassing little fool,' he groaned. 'You're not getting away with this.'

'Keep climbing, Gaff,' shouted Clementine, clinging onto his neck.

Gaff's fingers turned red as they strained to grip onto the fence. 'You're slipping!' he shouted. 'Hold on!'

'I can't,' Clementine said as Royce pulled at her body with all his might. 'I'm … losing … you!'

'Kick him!' screamed Allira. 'Kick as hard as you can!'

But with one final tug, Royce wrenched Clementine from Gaff's back. She fell onto the grass, winded and out of breath. Before she could get to her feet, Royce swept her up in his arms and threw her over his shoulder.

'Gotcha!' he said, punching the air in victory.

24.

An unwanted disguise

Melody's bedroom door burst open and her parents strode in again. They immediately locked the door behind them.

'What have you done?' Melody asked, leaping to her feet. 'Is Clementine alive?'

'Of course she's alive,' Mr Trumpet said, wiping crumbs from his lips. 'What do you take us for? We're not bad people.'

Mrs Trumpet, who had draped a fresh peacock-feather boa around her neck, pursed her lips. 'Relax. Royce has detained her and the gardener's brat in the dining room. They won't be blabbing to anyone.'

'But ... but Clementine fell out the window!' Melody said. 'How did she survive?'

'She's perfectly fine ... somehow,' Mr Trumpet said. 'Like I said, we're not bad people.'

Melody looked around her bedroom. The walls seemed to be edging closer to her. Her parents were keeping her and her friends prisoners. How could they not see that was bad?

'How do you know those two?' Mrs Trumpet demanded. 'Where did you come across people like … like that?'

'Like what?'

'People *like her*. The girl's hair is so knotted I wouldn't be surprised if an army of nits live in it!'

Melody glared at her mother, eyes blazing. 'Don't talk about Clementine like that. She's my friend.'

'You can't have friends,' Mrs Trumpet said. 'You have a big secret, one that you have to keep for all our sakes. Friends can talk. You don't want anything or anyone to get in the way of you and your reputation.'

'You mean *your* reputation. And I don't care about that any more. I care about Freddie and Clementine.'

Mr Trumpet chortled. 'You'll forget about them in a day or two when you get to your new school. You'll have everything you need there — and here's the best part: they don't teach music! No more pointless practice for you. In fact, they don't teach anything creative at all. And there are no expectations either, not at a school for the ordinary. Isn't that wonderful?'

Melody stared at the floor. 'But I won't have my friends.' Tears slid down her cheeks.

'Calm down, child,' her father said. 'You'll be a whole new person as soon as you get on that plane. You can pick whatever name you want for yourself — any name at all. You'll have the whole flight to think one up.'

Melody's tears turned to sobs.

'Do we need to sedate her?' Mrs Trumpet asked Mr Trumpet, her voice rising with panic.

'Viola! No! We … we … well, I don't know what to do. I thought this would be exactly what she wanted.'

'You're right, honey bear. It *is* what she wants. She just doesn't know it yet.' Mrs Trumpet turned to Melody. 'The media are still outside. We need a disguise for when you leave … and we need to do something with your hair. You can't look like … well, like Melody Trumpet any more. Barry, get Miss Sprinkles up here.'

'Miss Sprinkles doesn't know how to cut hair!' Melody said. 'She tried when I was little and it looked awful.'

'You're right,' Mrs Trumpet said. 'If anyone knows fashion and beauty in this manor, it's me.'

She took a pair of blunt silver scissors from the desk drawer and teetered towards Melody, the metal flashing in her hand. She snatched a section of Melody's thick ebony hair.

Snip.

Snip.

Snip.

Mrs Trumpet stepped back and admired her work. 'Well, I suppose it will do.'

More tears rolled down Melody's cheeks as the long strands of her hair fell to the floor.

* * *

'Keep your head down low,' Mrs Trumpet said, pulling Melody through the dark towards the limousine parked in the driveway. The media had dispersed hours ago but her parents were still worried about their plans being revealed.

Melody dragged her feet along the cement and her mother nudged her in the back. 'The faster we go, the faster this will be over. Then life can get back to normal for everybody.'

Melody grimaced. That wasn't true. Not now. Her fingers traced over the choppy, hacked edges of her new short haircut. This wasn't her normal at all. Even less normal was the fact that she was being pushed into the family limousine in the middle of the night and was about to be sent away to another country. And despite her parents trying to tell her this was an opportunity for a fresh start, she knew they were just forcing her to pretend to be something she wasn't. Again. She couldn't live another lie.

She could hear her parents whispering to each other. 'I'll get the decorators in tomorrow morning before the charity event kicks off in the afternoon,' Mrs Trumpet said. 'We'll jazz up that entire wing, maybe even knock out a wall or two. We can go big, Barry. Let's do something really special with the space and not let it go to waste any more.'

Melody's arms erupted into goosebumps in the cool night air and she came to a halt, fists clenched.

Mrs Trumpet didn't realise and walked into her. 'Heavens, child! Watch where you're going!'

'No,' Melody said, her voice shaking, 'enough of this pretending everything is fine. I'm not going any further until you tell me *exactly* what's going to happen to Freddie and Clementine.'

Mrs Trumpet narrowed her eyes at Melody's sudden defiance. 'We are doing all of this for you, you ungrateful child. And all you care about is those grotty little brats who broke into our beautiful home! Isn't our family important to you too? I mean ... you do love us, don't you?'

Melody didn't reply, biting her tongue to stop herself from blurting out the real question should really be whether her parents loved her.

Mrs Trumpet cleared her throat. 'It's better this way, I promise. Boarding school will be a good fit. You can be yourself there. Oh, and I organised something for you. Royce?'

Royce, wearing sunglasses despite the dark, handed Mrs Trumpet a present wrapped in a hot pink bow.

She thanked him and passed it to Melody. 'It's your dress from Claudette's. It's so spectacular I thought you couldn't bear to leave it behind.'

Melody shook her head in disbelief, too stunned to speak. She didn't want a reminder of her never-to-be Debut Gala performance.

'Better hop in,' Mrs Trumpet said, indicating the open car door. 'They're expecting you at the private runway anytime now.'

'And we're paying by the minute,' added Mr Trumpet with a chortle.

Gift box tucked under her arm, Melody glared inside the limousine. But there was nowhere to run, so she sighed and climbed into the back seat.

'Let's not make this farewell harder than it has to be,' Mr Trumpet said, peering through the door. 'We'll visit. At some point. Be sure to send us postcards.'

'The media attention will blow over soon and then we'll … we'll be in touch,' Mrs Trumpet said, pressing her icy fingers against Melody's cheek.

Melody shivered again. Partly from the cold. Partly because they were still lying to her. They wouldn't care if she sent them postcards. And they certainly wouldn't visit her. Before her parents could spit out another lie, Royce slammed the limousine door shut. Melody sat back in her seat, avoiding any further eye contact with her parents. She didn't look back as the limousine drove away.

If Melody ever wanted to see Freddie and Clementine again, it was up to her to find a way.

25.

Miss Sprinkles in charge

Inside Trumpet Manor, the smell of freshly baked choc-chip muffins wafted through the kitchen. Miss Sprinkles puffed her chest out in pride as she bent to take a peek in the oven, and smacked her lips at the sight. She slipped on a pair of oven mitts, removed the muffins from the oven and heaped them high onto a silver platter. She paused, then picked a daisy from the vase on the countertop and sat it on top.

'Perfect,' she murmured, before hurrying with the platter of muffins to the dining room. The door was locked, as Royce had ordered when he left to drive Melody to the airport, so Miss Sprinkles fetched the key from her apron pocket.

'Midnight snack, anyone?' she asked, opening the door and peering in.

Freddie and Clementine were seated on dining chairs, blindfolded and tied back to back with thick rope so they couldn't move their arms.

'Miss Sprinkles?' Freddie asked, squirming in his seat. 'Is that you? Don't you recognise me? It's Freddie! Morty Bloom's son.'

Miss Sprinkles tittered. 'That's a good one. Now, who's hungry?'

Clementine's stomach growled loudly. 'What do you think?' she replied.

'Well, you'll be happy to hear I added extra choc-chips,' Miss Sprinkles said. 'I always like cookies with extra choc-chips, don't you? I'll just leave the platter here on the table for you to enjoy.'

'Thanks,' Freddie said, giving Clementine's fingers a squeeze. 'But, ah ... maybe you could untie our arms so we can eat?'

'Silly me! Of course.' Miss Sprinkles hurried to their side. 'A choc-chip muffin, or three, always makes me feel better when I'm having a tough day. I do hope you enjoy — whoops!' She pulled her hand away from the rope with a laugh. 'You nearly got me!'

'So close to freedom,' Clementine murmured.

Freddie sighed. 'Yet so far.'

'If you stop being cheeky, I will remove your

188

blindfolds,' Miss Sprinkles said. 'You simply have to see the size of these choc-chips.'

She untied their blindfolds, and Freddie and Clementine blinked as their eyes adjusted to the light in the dining room. This time it was Freddie's stomach that rumbled.

'You *are* hungry!' Miss Sprinkles said. She picked up two muffins and held one to his mouth. 'Here, taste this prize-winning treat.' He took a big bite. 'Good, right?'

'Best I've ever had,' he said through a mouthful of muffin. 'Squishy and crunchy in all the right places. You're a genius.'

She blushed. 'You're just saying that.'

'No, really. You know … I … ah… I bet Melody loves your muffins too, Miss Sprinkles,' Freddie said, giving Clementine's fingers another gentle squeeze. 'She's really missing out by not being here.'

'She does love them!' Miss Sprinkles beamed, feeding him the rest of the muffin. 'And my scones too. I just hope they have a good cook at Dullard Private.'

'So that's the Trumpets' plan?' Clementine asked with a raised eyebrow. 'They're banishing her?'

'Ah … well … no, I didn't say that,' Miss Sprinkles stammered. 'Here, have a muffin.' She crammed the whole thing into Clementine's mouth.

Clementine bit down hard and managed to continue speaking with crumbs spraying everywhere. 'Delicious! So, ah ... if Melody loves your muffins so much, why isn't she here with us? Feels rude not to invite her, don't you think?'

'I would if I could — Melody loves a midnight snack, you know. But she's on her way to the private jet with Royce right now, off to boarding school overseas.'

Clementine gasped. 'Melody's already left? And the school is *overseas*?'

'Untie us ... please, Miss Sprinkles,' Freddie said. 'I ... I have to go to the bathroom. Badly. Right now!'

Miss Sprinkles shook her head. 'I'm not falling for that. Not after your other tricks.'

'At least let us help you with the washing up, Miss Sprinkles,' Clementine said, pinching Freddie's hand. 'I'm sure you have a kitchen full of dirty bowls and spoons, and it must get awfully tiring doing all the cleaning and cooking. I bet you often daydream about having an assistant to help.'

'You know what — I do,' Miss Sprinkles said. 'People just don't recognise hard work these days.'

'Well, tonight's your lucky night,' said Freddie. 'You've got two assistants right here.'

'We can get that kitchen looking spick and span,'

added Clementine. 'I mean, you work and you work and you work ...'

Miss Sprinkles beamed. 'Thank you for noticing. My feet are so sore after standing on them all day ... and, oh the bunions! A little help would come in handy.'

Freddie held his breath as Miss Sprinkles leaned close to Clementine, her hand resting on the rope.

But then she pulled away. 'Whoops! Silly me. Nearly fell for that too.'

She popped another muffin in each of their mouths, then tied the blindfolds around their eyes again. 'I suggest you stop playing games. Royce will be back from the airport soon, and once he is, he won't let you out of his sight.'

26.

Lost in Battyville

Nose pressed against the glass, Melody watched the night fly by as the limousine whizzed along dark streets. She struggled to see signposts and numbers — anything to pinpoint where they were.

The limousine turned one corner, then another, then so many that she was lost. Dejected, she traced a big loopy M in the mist on the window.

'Everything okay back there?' Royce asked, staring in the rear-view mirror and smacking his chewing gum. 'You're not smudging the glass, are you? I just got it washed.'

Melody avoided his steely gaze and stared at the street signs flashing by the window.

Jupiter Lane.

Spy Street.

Boffin Avenue.

She sat up a little straighter. They were on Clementine's side of town.

Humming to himself, Royce turned on the radio. 'Now, to show our respect for a very special family,' a deep throaty voice announced, 'here's a favourite. The number-one hit from the one and only ... Viola Trumpet.'

Melody stuffed her fingers in her ears, unable to bear hearing her mother's voice again that night.

Royce launched into a deep, out-of-key version of Mrs Trumpet's song. Melody wasn't sure who was the worse singer — herself or Royce.

She settled back into her seat as the limousine pulled up at a set of traffic lights. There were hardly any other cars around; just the occasional person cycling on the road or walking along the pavement.

By now Royce was screeching so loudly along with the radio that a thick vein pulsated in his neck. It looked like it might pop!

Melody's hand tightened around her backpack strap. Her gaze went to the limousine door handle, then to the empty street outside.

The traffic light was still red as Royce struggled to reach the highest of Mrs Trumpet's high notes, his eyes half-closed, his mouth open, spit spraying across the windscreen. This was Melody's chance.

She opened the limousine door and propelled herself through it. Royce yelled behind her, but she didn't turn around. She just ran.

Her breath was sharp and shallow as her feet pounded along the ground. Her backpack smacked against her side with every step. On she ran, with no idea where she was going. She darted down narrow streets, making sharp turns here and there. Eventually, after what seemed like forever, she lost Royce.

Gasping for breath, she slowed to a jog and turned down the next left turn in her path. A darkened alleyway.

'It's just a street,' she muttered. 'It's just the dark. I can do this.'

Like many people, she hated the dark. But she'd never been out in it before; she was always tucked up in her bedroom at night.

A pale white light shone at the end of the alleyway. She gritted her teeth, pulled her backpack in tight and aimed for it.

The hairs on her arms tingled at the pitter-patter of creatures scuttling around her and she jumped every time a dark shadow shifted. Sirens sounded somewhere nearby, then faded away as she headed deeper down the alleyway. She soldiered on towards the glimmering light ... and stepped face-first into a spiderweb!

Yelping in horror, she smoothed down her hair and clothes. 'It's just a spiderweb. I can do this.'

Melody bent down to pick up a jagged stick from the ground. Heart pounding, holding the stick out in front of her, she bolted to the end of the alleyway and into the light-filled street — where she slammed into a stocky man wearing a top hat and black leather boots. Melody dropped the stick in shock.

'Blimey,' the man said. 'Scared the life outta me. Stick or not, kiddo, you should know it ain't safe around these parts. You better scram.'

Melody hurried away down the street, which was lined with flickering fairy lights. She had no idea which way led home to Trumpet Manor — if she could even call it home any more. But that's where Freddie and Clementine were so she needed to get back to save them.

She looked to the left along the road. No cars. No people. No signs of life. She looked to the right. About the same, except for a black carriage and a large chestnut horse with a white mane tied to a lamppost.

The horse released a soft neigh as Melody stepped closer.

'You hungry, girl?' she asked. Its nostrils bristled and it pulled at its reins. Melody stuck out her hand and the horse sniffed on top, then underneath, before licking her fingertips. 'Hey, that tickles!'

She zipped open her backpack and rifled around inside before pulling out a slightly bruised banana. 'Snack time?' she asked. She began to peel it, but the horse chomped the whole banana out of her hand. Melody's stomach purred. 'Guess you're even hungrier than I am.'

'Oi, you there!' The stocky man was striding towards them. 'Thought I told you to scram, kiddo. Old Bertie don't like people.'

Melody stepped back. 'I'm sorry. She was hungry. I'm not trying to cause trouble.'

'What kid wandering the street alone after midnight *isn't* trying to cause trouble?'

'This one?' she replied.

The man's thin smile creaked into a grin that showed chipped yellow teeth. 'Righto. So what *do* you want? Money? 'Cos I don't have any.'

'No, not money.'

'Then what?'

'I … I don't know.'

'Well, while you work it out, I'll be on my way. Old Bertie here needs her beauty sleep.'

'Okay.' Melody stuffed her hands into her jacket pockets to try to warm up. Her fingers landed on something round and hard. She pulled it out. It was Clementine's gold coin from Town Square.

She held up the coin. 'Actually … do you know Trumpet Manor? Can you take me there?'

The man yawned. 'For one gold coin? You got a few more of those?'

Melody shook her head. 'I don't, but … but what about The Workshop? I think it's on Dreamboat Plaza. Wait, no — Dreamers Parade!'

The horse snuggled up to Melody, sniffing around her backpack, and she patted its mane.

'I told you, she don't like …' The man's voice trailed off as the horse whinnied in pleasure. 'Well, maybe Old Bertie does like *some* people. She's certainly taken to you.' He coughed. 'Alrighty, I don't know The Workshop but I can take you as far as the bottom of Dreamers Parade. Old Bertie won't be able to get you up the hill, not after the day we've had. Whaddya say?'

'Perfect.'

'And hang on to that gold coin. You might need it for luck.'

Melody gave the coin a squeeze before slipping it back into her pocket. 'Thank you.'

The man yawned again. 'Alright, let's go.'

Melody patted Old Bertie's mane once more, then hoisted herself up into the carriage.

'What's your name, by the way?' she asked the man. 'I won't forget this.'

He blushed, like someone hadn't asked him that question for years. 'First name's Pat. Last name's none of your business. How about you?'

She grinned. 'First name's Melody; last name's none of your business.'

Pat laughed. 'I see. Now hold your breath. Old Bertie's had her fair share of straw for dinner so she'll toot all the way there if I'm unlucky. And — this won't surprise you — I usually am.'

Right on cue, Old Bertie trumpeted from her magnificent rump!

Pat groaned, while Melody collapsed into a fit of giggles, laughing so hard that her cheeks hurt.

* * *

Fairy lights danced in the trees as Melody strode along Dreamers Parade. The street buzzed as people spilled out of restaurants and pubs after a night of merriment, jostling and laughing on their way home to bed before the sun rose. Melody asked everyone she passed if they knew where The Workshop was. Or whether they knew Mumma Rose? Or Clementine? Allira? Slack? Gaff?

Most people shook their heads, but occasionally someone waved her on with an encouraging smile.

'Keep going.'

'You're almost there, little one.'

'It's just up the hill.'

So up the hill she went. Her calves ached and her feet were beginning to blister, but Melody didn't slow down. She was determined to find her friends.

Before long, she was panting for breath on the path outside The Workshop. Ignoring the stitch in her belly, she hurried up the steps to the front door.

She knocked once.

Nothing.

Yawning, she knocked again.

Still nothing.

Again.

Nothing but the hum of Dreamers Parade.

Melody plopped down on the front step and leaned against the hard wooden door with a sigh. She closed her eyes, no longer able to fight sleep and too weary to remember Clementine's instructions to knock five times.

27.

The troupe step up

Melody squinted at the sunshine pouring through a window, and pulled a pillow over her head to block out the sound of birds chirping, muffled voices and a kettle whistling.

Wait, she thought, *where am I?*

She peered out from beneath the pillow. Then yelped as sharp teeth nipped her toes, which were poking out the end of the blanket. She sat up in shock and saw Moe curled up at the end of the bed.

'Moe!' She rubbed her eyes as he licked her big toe. 'What are you …? Where … where am I?'

Through tangled lashes, she soaked in her surroundings inside The Workshop: the row of empty single beds with mismatched blankets and pillows, the colourful artwork on the walls, the circus equipment, instruments and theatre props cluttering the dusty, scratched floorboards.

Her mind raced over the events of the previous night. Meeting Old Bertie. Finding Dreamers Parade. No one answering The Workshop's front door. Someone must have found her on the step and brought her inside!

Moe wagged his tail.

Melody stretched out her hand. 'Come here, boy. I know I'm not Clementine, but I promise we'll get her and Freddie back soon. My parents won't get away with this. Any of it.'

Whimpering, Moe buried his nose in the blanket.

'I'm sorry, Moe. I'm so tired of ruining everyone else's lives. Maybe it would be easier if I did just disappear like my parents want me to.'

Moe growled in disagreement and nudged his way into her arms.

'Don't worry,' she said, as Moe licked her on the nose. 'I'm not going anywhere. But I *do* need to put an end to this once and for all.'

Moe whimpered.

'I know, it's scary. I'm scared too. Once my secret is out, everything will change. I'll no longer be "the extraordinary Melody Trumpet". I'll just be … me. I don't know where I'll belong or what will happen. I just know I have to do it.'

She scratched Moe under the chin. 'Is Mumma Rose home?'

Moe barked twice and leaped off the bed, wagging his tail as a sign to follow him. Melody hurried after him as he scampered through The Workshop towards the kitchen.

They burst through the door to find Mumma Rose wrapped in a fluffy yellow dressing gown and sipping a steaming cup of tea. She was sitting in an old armchair covered in patches of different materials.

'Mumma Rose!' Melody blurted out. 'It's Clementine and Freddie ... I need your help! It's an emergency!'

'Good morning to you too, dear girl,' Mumma Rose said, peering over her glasses. She glanced at the clock. 'Well, almost good afternoon. I trust you slept better in bed than on our doorstep? Helga nearly tripped over you in the wee hours. Apparently she carried you inside and you didn't stir once.'

Unable to contain the swelling of emotion inside her chest, Melody threw her arms around Mumma Rose and cried into her dressing gown. Eventually, she wiped her wet nose and looked up at her, hoping for a miracle.

'I don't suppose Clementine is here too? And Freddie?'

'Nope, no sign of them,' Mumma Rose said.

202

Melody hung her head. 'Oh no ...'

'Allira, Slack and Gaff aren't here either. It's been quite a peaceful night without their buffoonery.'

'No, you don't understand — this is bad!' Melody said. 'And it's all my fault. I think they're in real trouble. We need to go to Trumpet Manor and save —'

Crash! The kitchen door burst open and Allira, Slack and Gaff tumbled inside, rolling into a heap on the floor.

'What in the ...' Mumma Rose said.

'Howdy,' Gaff said as Moe jumped all over them, licking their noses, their cheeks, even their shoes. 'How we all doing?'

'I've been better,' Mumma Rose said. 'Melody said we're in trouble. What's happened?'

'Oh, nothing much,' said Slack, wincing at a large purple bruise on his arm. 'Just your average failed-rescue-mission-turned-chase-scene-at-a-ginormous-manor. You know, standard stuff.'

'Freddie and Clementine were captured,' Allira explained. 'We were scaling a fence at the manor and — *bam!* Clementine got dragged back down.'

Mumma Rose covered her mouth in shock.

'This is awful. They must still be locked up inside the house,' Melody said, shaking her head. 'We need to go back for them.'

Allira did a double-take. 'Wait, I just realised. Melody, *you're here*! How did you escape?'

'It's a long story,' Melody told her.

'We stayed up all night trying to come up with a new rescue plan, but it got too dangerous,' said Gaff. 'We couldn't risk anyone else getting caught.'

Mumma Rose stamped her foot on the floor. 'I know it's been a wild night for everyone ... but what are you all talking about?!'

So Melody and the troupe filled her in: from the Trumpets' fake kidnapping of Melody and the one-way ticket to Dullard Private, to Clementine's and Freddie's attempt to save her, and her midnight escape from Royce through Battyville to Dreamers Parade.

'Now Clementine and Freddie are being held prisoner at Trumpet Manor,' Melody finished, her voice shaking. 'We have to rescue them. I have no idea what my parents are capable of any more. This secret has driven them mad!'

'What's our plan?' asked Gaff.

Melody swallowed. 'I'm not sure, but I can't stay here feeling helpless. We have to leave now! We'll work it out on the way.'

Mumma Rose patted Melody on the shoulder.

'You're a fighter, and Clementine is too.' Moe barked in agreement. 'She's tough, always had to be. Don't worry, we'll find her, and Freddie too.'

Melody sprang to her feet. 'Then let's go! Is your car parked outside?'

'The Workshop doesn't have cars,' Mumma Rose said. 'But we've all got legs for walking.'

'But that won't be fast enough. We need to get to the manor now!'

'If wheels are what you want, I have an idea.' Mumma Rose clapped her hands. 'Give us one minute. We'll meet you and Moe out the front. The Workshop sticks together, no matter what.'

* * *

Melody's jaw dropped at the sight of Mumma Rose, Allira, Slack and Gaff riding unicycles down Dreamers Parade!

'Ta da!' Mumma Rose announced as they came to a halt in front of The Workshop's front steps. 'Melody, you're riding on Gaff's shoulders.'

'Um ...' Melody looked up at Gaff's great height. He was wobbling on the spot too, which didn't ease her mind. 'Thanks, but ... ah ... maybe I'll jog or try to catch a bus or something.'

Mumma Rose and the others burst out laughing. 'Thought you might say that. Don't worry, you can ride the neighbour's bike.'

Mumma Rose pointed to a red bicycle with yellow streamers that was leaning against the neighbour's front gate. Melody walked over to it and studied its tyres. They looked a little worn and faded.

'Shouldn't we ask first?' she asked. 'I don't want to steal.'

'It's called "borrowing for an uncertain amount of time",' Mumma Rose said.

'We have an understanding around here,' Gaff said. 'What's ours is theirs, and vice versa.'

Melody bit her lip, then swung her leg over the seat. Her knuckles turned white as she gripped the handlebars, feet still firmly on the ground.

'You do know how to ride a bike, don't you?' asked Allira.

Melody blushed. 'Um ... sure.'

'Here,' said Slack, leaning down from his unicycle to pass Melody a glittery gold helmet. 'It's my favourite one. Hold on and we'll talk you through it.'

'Let's move it!' called Allira, taking off down the street. 'By the time we get over to the fancy-pants side of town, it'll be well into the afternoon.'

Her jaw hardening at the thought of Freddie and

Clementine being prisoners, Melody pushed down on the pedals. After a few shaky wobbles, she took off along the footpath. The troupe cheered.

'Look at you,' Mumma Rose sang out. 'You're a natural. See you'll get it —'

Melody began swaying from side to side, then crashed into a row of rubbish bins.

Mumma Rose tried not to laugh. 'Eventually.'

28.

The Charity Gala

Principal Sharp adjusted her glasses, which were already perfectly placed on her thin nose. She smoothed down her hair, which was slicked into a tight bun on top of her head. If she could have straightened her back any more she would have, but she was already as rigid as a ruler. She peeked out from behind the curtain. People were streaming into Crescendo Hall to pay their respects to the Trumpets at the Charity Gala. She sucked in a breath, then flattened down her pencil skirt, even though there wasn't a crease or crinkle to be seen.

'Allegra,' said a man behind her.

Principal Sharp turned to see Mr Pizzicato in the wings.

'You're back,' she whispered. 'You're here.'

They shared a stiff hug, which was all pointed elbows and sharp angles.

'I came as soon as I saw the news about Melody,' he said. 'I'll be cheering on Clive the Chicken. He's just brushing his feathers and practising his vocal warm-ups in his dressing room. Such a perfectionist.'

'Oh, poor Melody — alone, kidnapped. She must be petrified,' Principal Sharp said, wringing her hands. 'It's so terrible for the Trumpets, for the school, for the town.'

'The poor girl,' Mr Pizzicato said, hanging his head. 'But what a heartening turnout for the Charity Gala. And have you seen all the cameras?'

'I've lost track of the number of television crews that have arrived. International reporters too,' Principal Sharp said, sniffing into a tissue. 'It's all so unbelievable.'

'Yes, unbelievable indeed ...' Mr Pizzicato's voice trailed off as he looked through a gap in the curtain. The Trumpets were seated in the front row beside the Prince and Princess of Zanjia. Their Royal Highnesses were draped in exquisite silk attire in the boldest of purples and blues, and their gold crowns were adorned with glittering diamonds and sapphires.

Mrs Trumpet was dressed head to toe in black, with a lace fascinator perched on her head like a bird's nest, and a feather boa wrapped around her neck. Mr Trumpet was in his best white shirt, suspenders and red pants.

'The timing is particularly strange,' Mr Pizzicato added.

'What do you mean?' Principal Sharp asked, eyebrow raised.

'Nothing,' he said. But he clearly didn't mean it. 'It's just ... why are the Trumpets here if Melody isn't? We should all be out looking for her.'

A young man hurried to Principal Sharp's side, interrupting their conversation. He swept a make-up brush over her cheeks to add a tinge of pink. 'Got to make those gorgeous eyes of yours pop,' he said, flashing her a wink. 'We're streaming this event live on television so you'll want to look your best!'

Principal Sharp shooed him away and turned back to Mr Pizzicato. 'Is there something you want to tell me?'

Mr Pizzicato drew in a deep breath and opened his mouth ... just as a loud bell rang through the hall.

'Shoot,' Principal Sharp said. 'That's my cue.'

Lips pursed, she walked across the stage and took her place behind a lectern. She cleared her throat once. Twice. Three more times.

The audience adjusted their positions in their seats, partly out of discomfort, partly to fill in the awkward silence. There wasn't a spare seat in the crowd. A pack of camera crews swarmed in front of the stage, while a group of reporters hovered in the opposite corner.

'Good afternoon, everyone,' Principal Sharp said at last. 'And a big Battyville Elite School For Musically Gifted Children welcome to all of you.' She paused and straightened the lectern unnecessarily. 'Thank you for coming today. As you all know, we have had to cancel the annual Debut Gala, and instead are here to raise money and awareness for a very special cause. Melody Trumpet, the only daughter of alumni and patrons of the arts Viola and Barry T Trumpet, has been kidnapped.'

Cries rang out around the room.

'Kidnapped!'

'That poor girl!'

'So it's true!'

'Heartbreaking! A travesty!'

'What can we do?'

'Let's start a search party!'

'Silence!' Principal Sharp said, tapping her microphone. The vibrations reverberated around the room. 'Melody is still missing but we must not panic.'

The room was silent. Not a word nor a whisper, nor a sneeze nor a sniffle.

'The police believe this to be a ransom situation due to the Trumpets' high standing in our society,' she continued. 'They hope to receive instructions on what to do next very soon. But please know, everyone is focused on getting Melody home safe and sound.

'Now please welcome our first performer to the stage: the remarkable, the accomplished, the phenomenal … Clive the Chicken!'

The audience clapped as Clive strutted onto the stage and took his spot on a red velvet cushion in front of a short microphone. As his faultless soprano voice soared through the speakers, Principal Sharp hurried backstage and patted her forehead and cheeks with a tissue.

The make-up artist popped up beside her again. 'Got to keep you looking glamorous for the cameras,' he said, ignoring her glare as he powdered her nose. 'This'll be a ratings bonanza.'

'It … it will?' she replied, smoothing back her tight bun, which still didn't need to be smoothed.

'You bet. The circumstances aren't great, but trust me — the Trumpets are in the spotlight. They'll be on the cover of every newspaper and magazine! You won't be able to leave your house without seeing their faces on a billboard.'

'Really?'

'Don't take my word for it,' the make-up artist said, sweeping more blush onto her cheeks. 'Look around — Viola and Barry T Trumpet won't have seen this level of media attention for years. It's the biggest story in the world right now.'

29.

To Crescendo Hall

Melody skidded her bicycle to a halt in front of Battyville Electrical. Its colourful window display was buzzing with *Sale!* signs and televisions of different sizes. Her jaw dropped at the words running across the bottom of each screen:

TRUMPET HEIR KIDNAPPED!

PRINCE AND PRINCESS LAUNCH CAMPAIGN TO BRING MELODY HOME

DEBUT GALA CANCELLED! CHARITY FUNDRAISER AT HEIR'S SCHOOL

Melody waved the others over. 'Check this out!'

'Kidnapped? Is there a financial reward if we hand you in?' Allira joked, hopping off her unicycle to get a better look.

'Put a stinky sock in it!' Slack hissed at her.

'She's kidding,' Gaff said, winking at Melody.

Footage of the Trumpets at last night's press conference played on the screens and Melody had to watch her mother's performance all over again.

'All these lies because they're too scared to tell the truth,' she said, pressing a hand against the glass.

'Fear makes people do strange things, dear girl,' Mumma Rose said.

The screens showed a sweeping shot across a sombre audience squeezed into Crescendo Hall. Mouth covered in shock, Melody watched as her parents walked into the hall and were pulled into warm embraces by the Prince and Princess of Zanjia. They dabbed at their eyes with hankies, then took their seats in the front row.

'It's my parents' charity event,' she cried. 'And it's live! Quick, follow me!'

She hurried into the store and the others followed her. They all crowded around a display of televisions in a corner.

'What are we looking at?' whispered Allira to Slack.

'I don't know,' he replied. 'But I don't want to miss a second.'

Mrs Trumpet batted her thick eyelashes at a camera that zoomed in for a close-up. A single tear rested on her cheek. Perhaps it wasn't powered by enough emotion to roll all the way down, Melody thought.

Together, her mother and father stood and walked up onto the stage and to the lectern. Mr Trumpet kept his gaze low the whole way.

After another long, eyelash-batting look to the camera, Mrs Trumpet pressed her plump lips close to the microphone. 'First, thank you to everyone who's travelled to be here, especially the Prince and Princess for their presence and most generous contribution.'

The Princess bowed her head in the front row.

Mrs Trumpet's voice trembled as she went on. 'We were so looking forward to Melody performing for you all after all these years. To have her disappear in such *mysterious* circumstances is so unfortunate. She'd been practising day in, day out, and we had the most perfect event planned. Instead, we now have a solemn concert to bring everyone together in the hope of finding our poor daughter.' She whimpered, before adding in a rush, 'And don't forget to buy my latest "Best Of Viola Trumpet" album, which will be released in stores tomorrow. One per cent of the profits will go towards finding Melody and bringing her home.'

'She is unbelievable,' Mumma Rose said, and Moe barked twice in agreement.

Melody's jaw hardened as she watched her mother swan around the stage, swooning over her beautiful, missing daughter. She wished she was surprised by it all, but nothing her parents did could surprise her now.

She turned away from the screen to find everyone's eyes on her.

'Are you okay?' Allira asked. 'Sorry, I don't know what else to say.'

'Then don't say anything,' Slack told her, wrapping an arm around Melody's shoulders.

Suddenly Melody gasped. 'Surely not ...' she murmured, stepping closer to the television to get a better look.

Melody squinted, unsure if she was imagining things. A bulky red-faced man who looked suspiciously like Royce was sneaking along the back of Crescendo Hall with two people wriggling and writhing across his broad shoulders. A girl and a boy. They were handcuffed, blindfolded and had tape stuck across their mouths, but Melody recognised the fiery red braid and shaggy brown hair. It was Clementine and Freddie!

'Look, it's them!' Melody shouted, pressing her finger against the screen. 'I think it's them!'

The troupe gasped and huddled in closer.

'Clem! Our poor girl!' cried Mumma Rose, gnawing at her fingernail as she watched the footage. 'Where is that awful man taking them?'

216

Melody wished she had the answer. She bit her bottom lip but it didn't calm her racing mind — she had no idea what Royce and her parents planned to do to her friends.

The footage on screen was cutting between different parts of the Charity Gala, from the dazzling dramatics on stage to the besotted audience. It was clear no one there had noticed Clementine and Freddie squirming on Royce's shoulders as he lumbered towards a side door up the back. The audience was too transfixed by Mrs Trumpet's teary performance that was intended to 'pay tribute to little Melody' to see anything else.

Royce appeared to be hobbling under the combined weight of Freddie and Clementine as he fumbled at the door's handle, but he managed to open it and they disappeared through it into the main area of the school.

Melody knew what they should do next.

'Forget Trumpet Manor,' she said, clenching her fists. 'If my parents are at Crescendo Hall, Royce won't be leaving anytime soon. He's their bodyguard and driver — where they go, he goes. We have to get to the school right now and save Clementine and Freddie!'

30.

The truth is out

'Which way to the hall, Melody?' asked Mumma Rose
as they entered the winding corridors of Battyville Elite
School For Musically Gifted Children. 'Right, left or
straight ahead?'

Everyone looked at Melody.

'I have no idea,' she said. 'I was banned from this
part of the school. Um ... let's go right ...'

Moe suddenly wriggled in Gaff's arms and delivered
three barks in quick succession, tail wagging with
excitement.

'He's found something,' Slack said.

'What is it, boy?' asked Allira, scratching Moe under
the chin.

'Is it Clementine?' Melody asked. 'Can you take us
to her and Freddie?'

Moe leaped from Gaff's arms and sniffed along the

carpet, before barking three times at something small and silver on the ground. Everyone rushed over to see what he'd found.

A button.

'It's Clementine's,' Mumma Rose said, picking it up and putting it in her pocket. 'From her overalls. Quick, Moe, lead the way!'

Moe whined, and bolted off around a corner. The troupe chased after him, turning left, turning right, winding their way through the corridors. They passed classroom after classroom, hurried through a tree-lined quadrangle, then raced up a set of steps and burst through double doors that led to ... another corridor.

'This is hopeless,' Melody said. 'Where *are* they?'

Moe barked again and trotted further along the corridor. Its walls were lined with enormous framed portraits of the Trumpets at various points in their illustrious careers, from a black-and-white photo of Mr Trumpet conducting a one-thousand-person orchestra, to a heavily pregnant Mrs Trumpet singing at the former Prime Minister's sixtieth birthday party. Melody groaned and hurried after Moe, shaking off the feeling of being spied on by her parents.

The little dog led the group to a closed door with a sign that read *Cafeteria* and began scratching at the floorboards.

'Get back, Moe,' whispered Melody as the others pressed in tight around her. 'We're doing this in ... three, two ...'

'One!' everyone shouted in unison as Gaff kicked down the door and they burst into the cafeteria.

'What in the ...?' Royce shouted.

He jumped to his feet, spilling jam from the doughnut he was eating down his shirt, and ran over to stand guard in front of Freddie and Clementine, who were handcuffed to a thick pipe in the corner.

'You came!' cried out Freddie.

'Our heroes!' Clementine cheered. 'Told you they'd find us, Freddie.'

'Miss us or something?' Allira smirked.

She stretched one long leg up around her neck, then performed ten perfect aerial cartwheels to land right in front of Royce. His eyes widened in surprise.

'Here we go!' Clementine said, laughing. 'It's showtime.'

Slack flexed his muscles, did three double backwards somersaults towards Royce, then grabbed six bowling pins from his backpack. He tossed them to Mumma Rose, who juggled them as she pirouetted with the others to surround Royce. Allira twirled and swirled her rhythmic gymnastics ribbon through the air, whipping and cracking it to give Royce a fright. Gaff, who had been guarding the door, pulled out his torch and set it alight, then stormed towards the group in a flurry of fiery flames.

'Please don't hurt me,' Royce cried, cowering against the pipe as Allira's ribbon licked at his calves.

Within seconds, Allira and Slack had overpowered him and tied him to the pipe. He strained and tugged, but was trapped.

Gaff plucked the half-eaten jam doughnut from the nearby table and popped it into Royce's mouth.

Not to be left out of the fun, Moe trotted over to Royce, lifted one leg and widdled on his trousers!

'Being captured doesn't feel so good, does it?' Clementine said to Royce. 'Meanwhile, hint, hint, you lot!' She and Freddie jangled their handcuffed wrists against the pipe. 'Mumma Rose, grab a bobby pin from my hair to work your magic.'

'On it,' Mumma Rose said. She fished out a pin from Clementine's braid, and jiggled it around in the handcuffs until they unlocked.

* * *

Gaff peeked through another door before closing it with a disappointed sigh. 'Nope, not the exit. Just a store room, although it's about as big as The Workshop,' he announced. 'So if the cafeteria is back down the corridor to the left then that must mean we're ... well ...'

'Lost?' Allira suggested with a grin.

'So much for retracing our steps,' added Mumma Rose.

Melody exhaled. 'Are you sure you don't know how to get out of here, Freddie? You come here every day.'

'It's a labyrinth.' Freddie shrugged. 'My classes are on the east side of the grounds, too – this is my first time on the west!'

The troupe dawdled along, opening doors and peeking out windows to look for any familiar locations. Allira was the first to reach a wide mahogany door with brass handles.

'This looks promising,' she said to the troupe. 'Maybe it could get us out of this enormous place?'

'Maybe.' Freddie shrugged again. 'Or it could be a broom closet.'

'You open it, Slack,' urged Allira. 'What if it's the principal's office?'

Slack elbowed her. 'You open it!'

While the twins squabbled, Melody rolled her eyes and turned the handle.

They all bowled through the door — into darkness. Melody bumped into something tall and spindly, and before she knew it the others had knocked into her and they were all twisted up in a large sheet of velvet. With an almighty crash and a clatter, they fell into a heap in the blackness. Panicked screaming echoed somewhere in the distance.

'My legs are caught!' Gaff said to the group.

'Same,' groaned Allira. 'What *is* this thing? Move it, Slack!'

'Freddie, you go left, I'll go right,' Clementine said.

'Everyone, calm down,' Mumma Rose chimed in.

'But, Mumma Rose, I can't see —'

'What's going on here?' another voice asked. 'Who are you all?'

'Mr Pizzicato?'

'*Melody?*'

'Yes! And you're back from your holiday!'

'I think it's a big curtain,' Allira said. 'The velvet is tickling my skin.'

'Well, if there's a big velvet curtain, we must be —'

A bright white light suddenly shone down on them.

'Alien invasion! There's no other explanation.'

'Allira, stop it! I'll take a look.' Slack peeped out into the light, then dived back under the curtain. 'Ah, heads-up,' he whispered. 'We didn't find the exit ... we found Crescendo Hall! The back of the stage to be more specific.' He noticed a dazed Mr Pizzicato twisted up in their mess. 'Wait, who's this guy?'

223

The curtain began to slip off them and they all saw Clive the Chicken trembling at the front of the stage, shedding feathers with every distressed cluck and squawk.

'Whoa, is that Clive the Chicken?' Slack asked. 'We should get his autograph!'

By now, Melody, Mr Pizzicato and the troupe had struggled free of the curtain, revealing their identities to the audience packed into the hall.

Principal Sharp gasped.

Mr and Mrs Trumpets' faces were frozen with shock.

'It's her! The girl!' someone cried.

'Can't be — she's got short hair.'

'It is! It's Melody Trumpet! And they must be her abductors! They've come to kill us all! Run, everyone!'

Shrieking ripped through Crescendo Hall as people ran for the exits. Melody could hear Mr Pizzicato and Principal Sharp shouting, 'Stay calm!', but no one seemed to be listening. Camera crews jostled for the best positions to capture the chaos.

'Oh no,' Melody muttered, taking in the pandemonium.

Only Mr Bloom and Freddie's younger siblings were still in their seats, their jaws dropped. Even the Trumpets were trying to flee, but they were hampered by being in the front row.

A swarm of police officers surrounded the stage, making sure that Melody and the troupe couldn't escape.

'Don't just stand there!' shrieked the Princess. 'Arrest the kidnappers!'

The officer in charge signalled to his team to block off the exits. 'Everyone, stay in your seats,' he shouted. 'It's for your own safety.'

The Trumpets slunk back down in their seats in the front row. The Prince demanded answers of the police officer in charge, while the Princess stared in disbelief at the curious-looking troupe on stage.

'This is outrageous!' Mumma Rose told the officers. 'Let us go!'

'What do they think we're going to do?' Slack asked Allira. 'Cartwheel them to death?'

The police officers closed in further. 'We don't want any funny business,' one of them said. 'We're just here for the girl.'

'I'm fine! I'm not hurt!' Melody said, her voice shaking a little. 'These are my friends. They tried to save me from ... well ...'

Whispers echoed through the remaining audience members as Melody sucked in a deep breath, walked over to Clive the Chicken and plucked the microphone from the stand in front of him. He clucked with displeasure.

'There are criminals here,' Melody continued, her voice booming out across the hall, 'and they've been lying to everyone. They're my parents — Viola and Barry T Trumpet!'

The audience muttered in confusion.

'The Trumpets are crooks?'

'This must be a joke! Are we being pranked?'

'Madness, all of it!'

Clementine, Freddie, Mumma Rose and the rest of the troupe lined up on either side of Melody. The police officers dropped back a little.

Melody looked at her parents. They were sinking lower into their seats and wouldn't meet her gaze.

'My name is Melody ...' She cleared her throat. 'My name is Melody Trumpet, heir of the Trumpet empire, and despite what you've all been told for the past ten years, I'm not who my parents said I am.'

Mrs Trumpet's nervous laughter ricocheted around the hall. She pulled Mr Trumpet up from his seat by his suspenders. 'If you'll just excuse us,' she said, forcing a fake smile for the cameras. 'There seems to be a tiny mistake —'

'Stay in your seat, ma'am,' ordered the senior police officer. He gestured to two of his officers to guard each end of the Trumpets' row. 'We're not done here.'

Melody's cheeks were flushed pink as she went on with her speech. 'For ten years, I've been separated from you all,' she said, her voice growing stronger. 'Thanks to my parents' lies, you believed I was special. A musical genius. A prodigy. *Extraordinary.*' Her lip quivered. 'But none of it is true. I can't sing, or play an instrument, or do any of the amazing things you think I can do.'

Outraged cries filled the hall.

'My parents are the real kidnappers,' Melody said, pointing at them. 'They locked me in my bedroom, captured my friends and faked this whole thing. *They're* the real criminals!'

The room erupted as people shouted and gasped at Melody's accusation. The police moved in on the Trumpets, handcuffs at the ready. The camera crews looked ready to explode with excitement as they surged forward to get the best shot of the Trumpets being arrested.

Melody raised her voice to be heard over the uproar. 'The truth is: I'm just ordinary. And you know what? I'm fine with that.'

She bent to put down the microphone, but Clementine stepped forward, wrapped one arm around Melody's shoulders, and took the microphone with her spare hand.

227

'Sorry to interrupt, everyone, I just need to correct something,' Clementine said. 'Um, so Melody hasn't been entirely truthful with you all.'

The audience broke out into angry shouts again. Melody looked at Clementine in shock.

'Yes, the Trumpets are criminals,' Clementine continued, tugging at her overalls, which were slipping due to the missing button. 'They've been lying to the world, and they orchestrated this whole disaster to cling to their fame. But Melody told you that she isn't extraordinary, that she's not someone special. Well, that's not true at all! Sure, she can't sing opera like her mother, or conduct an orchestra like her father ... but who cares? Those are *their* things. And if her parents had taken one minute to get to know their daughter, they would have discovered what we here from The Workshop knew from the beginning: Melody loves to write. So what if she can't sing or play the piano or the flugelhorn ... *she can write.* It's not in her fancy Trumpet blood ... but it's in her heart.'

The audience had fallen silent. Even the police officers surrounding the Trumpets held their collective breath until Clementine spoke again.

'Melody Trumpet *is* extraordinary. Because there's nothing more extraordinary than taking the time to work out what it is that makes *your* heart sing.'

The crowd leaped to their feet and burst into wild applause.

'I'm sorry to take over proceedings,' Clementine said, shooting a bashful grin at Principal Sharp, 'but I believe you were promised a debut performance by Melody Trumpet. Well, we're here to deliver it by performing one of Melody's original songs on her behalf. Our dear friend Freddie Bloom will also be making his debut.'

31.

Under the spotlight

What happened next was like a dream for Melody.

Mumma Rose directed the troupe into a semi-circle on stage behind Clementine as she centred herself at the microphone stand. Freddie dashed off stage into the wings and emerged moments later holding a brown classical guitar. Melody stepped aside, eager to escape the spotlight, but Clementine's hand found hers and drew her back to her side. Melody's palm was clammy from nerves, but Clementine didn't let go.

'You should be so proud,' Clementine whispered. 'Don't forget that.' She turned to Freddie with a toothy grin. 'Debut time, kid.'

He nodded, guitar pick between his teeth as he tuned the strings.

Clementine murmured, 'Five, six, seven, eight ...' to Freddie, then brought the microphone to her lips.

Waiting and hoping,
For someone to see,
The girl in the tower,
And what she could be.

But life just goes on,
And things stay the same,
So from a distance she watches,
Away from the game.

Clementine's eyes were closed as her right boot tapped to the beat – and her fingers stayed entwined with Melody's through every word of the song. The troupe swayed from side to side in unison, harmonising with Clementine's vocals to create a beautifully rich and textured sound that rang clear through Crescendo Hall.

Melody watched in awe as Freddie's fingers danced up and down the neck of the guitar, performing music gymnastics on the strings. She noticed a soft blush reddening his cheeks and followed his gaze deep into the audience to see Mr Bloom and Freddie's siblings waving from their row. His father shot him an encouraging thumbs-up as Freddie rocked out on stage, proving to everyone at Battyville Elite School

For Musically Gifted Children that he deserved to be there just as much, if not more, than them.

Yet one day she's certain,
That someone will see,
The girl in the tower,
And what she will be.

Thunderous applause filled the room after the final strains of Melody's song faded away. People shouted 'Encore!' until their throats burned.

But Mr and Mrs Trumpet stayed slumped in their seats throughout the entire performance, too shocked to move at the news Melody had been writing lyrics all this time.

On stage, Mr Pizzicato walked over to Melody, Freddie and Clementine. 'Marvellous work,' he said. 'All of you. The arrangement. The harmonies. And, Melody, the words were ... well, quite simply beautiful.'

Melody bit her lip. 'Thanks, Mr P.'

'I'm so sorry for failing you, my dear,' he said, dabbing at his wet eyes with his shirt-sleeve. 'I missed the very thing that makes you ... well, you. Songwriting! It must have been the only thing we didn't try.'

'It's okay,' Melody said.

'Your friends are right: you *are* extraordinary, and

I'm sorry I never helped you understand that. My only solace is that you learned this valuable lesson despite my carelessness. Can you ever forgive me?'

'Of course.' Melody squeezed Mr Pizzicato's arm. 'As long as you never make me play the flugelhorn again.'

They grinned at each other.

The sounds of an enormous party swelled around them, until suddenly the crowd's joyous cheers were replaced by shrieks.

Melody turned to see her parents wrestling with the police officers. Feathers and pearls were flying everywhere!

'Somebody stop them!' cried someone in the audience. 'They're trying to flee!'

'Liars! Fakes!' shouted someone else.

Mr Trumpet managed to get two officers in a headlock, one under each arm. Mrs Trumpet tickled another two officers with her feather boa and wriggled free from their attempt to put her in handcuffs.

Panting and screeching, Melody's parents made a beeline straight for their daughter on the stage.

'Our beautiful, talented, *extraordinary* child,' whimpered Mrs Trumpet, her mascara smeared down her cheeks, her once-perfect chignon bun collapsed into a frizzy mess.

'I suggest you leave her alone, ma'am,' Mr Pizzicato said, stepping in front of Melody. 'Surely enough damage has been done.'

'It's alright, Mr P,' Melody said. 'I can handle this.'

Mrs Trumpet shot a dark look at Mr Pizzicato. 'You traitor!' she hissed, before turning back to Melody with a huge, false smile. Melody could see lipstick smudged on her front teeth. 'How the people love you, my little cream puff. You're a star! A real Trumpet now.'

Melody's jaw hardened. 'No, Mother, I'm still me. You just never saw me before.'

'Let's not worry about the details. The important thing is we finally have a worthy heir,' boomed Mr Trumpet, pinching Melody on the cheek. 'The Trumpet empire is complete. I say we get Royce to bring the limousine around to collect us. This calls for a celebration.'

Melody didn't bother mentioning that Royce was currently tied up with Allira's rhythmic gymnastics ribbon in the school cafeteria.

'And another press conference, Barry,' Mrs Trumpet said, fluffing her hair. She turned to the audience. 'Who wants to interview me about Melody? I always believed she would prove her worth to the world one day. Also, don't forget my album goes on sale tomorrow —'

'Stop right there!' cried the senior police officer. He and his officers circled the Trumpets and handcuffed them. 'Viola and Barry T Trumpet, you're under arrest for fraud and kidnapping.'

Mr Trumpet burst into tears and blubbered for his mummy.

Mrs Trumpet promised to give every police officer a signed copy of her entire music collection if they let her go. When her pleas were ignored, she turned to the nearest TV camera with bloodshot eyes. 'You won't forget this — you won't forget us!' she spat out. 'Everyone will remember the Trumpet name for as long as they live.'

She wasn't wrong about that, Melody thought.

'Let's get out of here,' Mumma Rose said, and Moe barked in agreement.

'You read my mind,' Melody said.

She walked down the stage steps with Clementine and Freddie and The Workshop troupe, ignoring the crowd's requests for hugs, autographs and photos.

Someone shrieked her name over the din. A news reporter with a slimy smirk and a cameraman in hot pursuit appeared in front of her. 'You're on live television, Melody! Can I ask you a few questions?'

'No, thanks,' she said, walking past them. 'We're leaving.'

'But this is your day,' said the reporter, chasing her with the microphone. 'How does it feel to be —'

'You heard her, she said no!' Freddie said to him. 'Now back off.'

The reporter snorted. 'But it's the Melody Trumpet show. Melody, everyone is here at Crescendo Hall for *you*. Isn't this what you always dreamed of? Attention, fame, your name in lights?'

Melody stopped and crinkled her nose. 'No. Not at all. In fact, sometimes ...'

Her voice trailed off as she watched the police take away her handcuffed parents. Her father was sobbing onto an officer's shoulder, while her mother warbled one of her famous arias to the cameras. Her final performance before the police locked them up and threw away the key.

'Sometimes people need to be careful what they wish for,' Melody finished.

With that, she marched towards the exit, her gaze locked straight ahead. Moe trotted along at her side, and her friends somersaulted, cartwheeled and juggled behind her.

32.

The perfect place

'Now what?' Freddie asked when they reached the school gates. 'Back to Trumpet Manor?'

Melody rolled her eyes. 'Not yet. Not after being cooped up in my bedroom for days.'

'Just kidding,' he said. 'Although the entire place *is* yours now. And I used to think having a wing to yourself was cool.'

Gaff raised an eyebrow. 'Think of the parties you can throw.'

'Don't forget the swimming pool,' said Slack.

'And the menagerie,' Allira added. 'I've always wanted to cuddle a llama, and you have five!'

'We'll enjoy it all, I promise, but first ... I have an idea,' Melody said. She hopped onto the bicycle.

'Wait, you can ride a bike now?' Clementine asked, with a twinkle in her eye. 'And did you steal that?'

'That haircut really *has* changed you,' Freddie said.

'No, I just borrowed it for an uncertain amount of time,' Melody said, trading grins with Mumma Rose. 'Follow me, everyone!'

Together, they travelled through the streets of Battyville — Freddie on his skateboard, Mumma Rose, Allira, Gaff and Slack on their unicycles, Clementine balanced on Slack's shoulders with Moe in her arms — until they arrived at Melody's destination: Clementine's favourite spot in the centre of Town Square.

'Home, sweet home,' Clementine said. 'Nice choice, kid. But I don't have my guitar.'

'And I don't have my keyboard,' Freddie added.

'You told me anything can work if we do it together,' Melody said. 'So let's do it with just voices, a cappella, and make it the ultimate Workshop performance.'

'Thought you'd never ask,' Slack said. 'Everyone in position!'

Gaff cracked his neck, Allira did some quick stretches and Mumma Rose fished out her juggling balls.

'Wait, which song?' asked Freddie. 'Weren't you working on a new one?'

Melody smiled, remembering him hiding the piece of paper in his mouth. There hadn't exactly been time to polish the new words since then!

'Let's go with what I scribbled down at The Workshop,' she said.

'Perfect,' Mumma Rose said, giving Melody's hand a squeeze. 'A full circle.'

Clementine waved over a few people wandering through Town Square. 'Ladies and gentlemen, it's my honour to stand here before ... well, nine of you.' She gestured to another group, calling them to join the audience. 'This is an exclusive unplugged performance so come in closer, folks. You don't want to miss a thing.'

'Actually, this was a bad idea,' Melody whispered to Freddie. 'What was I thinking?'

'We're all here,' he said. 'It'll be fun, remember?'

The audience had swollen to about fifty people, thanks to Allira twirling one of her ribbons while she balanced on Slack's shoulders.

Clementine clapped her hands to get everyone's attention. 'This is a song written by the one and only Melody Trumpet — the girl who puts the *extraordinary* in ordinary.' She winked at Melody. 'A one, a two, a one, two, three, four ...'

Here we are,
Just us four ...

'Oops, sorry Melody, there're eight of us now!'

Hours in the sun,
Together on this day ...

As always, Clementine sang vocals with Moe by her side; Freddie was on percussion, hitting the cobblestones with two sticks, and singing back-up; while Mumma Rose, Allira, Slack and Gaff formed a juggling, ribbon-twirling, fire-breathing circle around them.

How long I have dreamed,
For a place such as this,
Where time disappears,
And adventure can begin.

Melody's heart beat faster as she murmured the words to herself, humming along with Clementine's ethereal vocals.

It was all messy and new,
They smiled so I smiled too ...

'Shall we do the last bit together?' Clementine whispered to Melody out of the corner of her mouth as the crowd clapped at Allira's backflip off Slack's shoulders. 'Only if you want to.'

'I don't know …' Melody swallowed. 'What if I make a mistake?'

But then she remembered Clementine's words from the other day: *We'll keep going with their laughter ringing in our ears.*

Melody looked at the crowd in Town Square. There were no judgmental looks, cruel sniggers or disappointed faces. There was nothing to be afraid of.

'I'm in,' she said, her face cracking into a beaming smile. For once, she could be herself without letting down her parents or getting in trouble. Flawed, *extraordinarily* imperfect Melody.

'Ready?' Freddie asked.

'Nope. Not at all. But you know what, Freddie Bloom, after everything we've been through, I'll survive.'

With her eyes closed and mouth wide open, Melody sang the words that she'd never dared to sing before:

Everything to gain,
And nothing to prove,
On this day.

Her voice squeaked and croaked like always, but she didn't mind. She was lost in the feeling, and her heart thumped to the beat of coins raining onto the concrete.

She had found somewhere to belong.

The kind of place that was in her head ...

The perfect place for her.

Acknowledgments

First, a huge thanks to the HarperCollins dream team: Lisa Berryman, Cristina Cappelluto, Eve Tonelli, Nicola O'Shea, Michelle Weisz, Georgia Williams, Jacqui Barton, Kady Holt and Pam Dunne. A special shoutout also goes to illustrator Risa Rodil for bringing my beloved Melody to life on the cover in such a clever and charming way.

To all my favourite people, including my family, friends and readers: you're the best cheerleaders a writer could ask for. I adore going on this creative ride with you all and can't wait for our next adventure together. Much love to Mum and Dad for their continuous support, especially during the race towards the finish line.

And, as always, here's looking at my first reader: JT. It's no exaggeration to say I wouldn't have finished the first draft of this novel without your patience, feedback and strawberry Freddo Frog snack runs. Sienna and I are so lucky to have such a kind and imaginative soul in our lives.

Gabrielle Tozer is an award-winning and internationally published author and freelance writer based in Sydney, Australia. She has published five books, including the young adult novels *Remind Me How This Ends* (which was on the Children's Book Council of Australia's 2018 Notable list and longlisted for the 2018 Gold Inky Award), *Faking It* and *The Intern*, which won the 2015 Gold Inky Award.

Her first picture book, *Peas and Quiet* (illustrated by Sue deGennaro), was published in 2017, as was her young-adult short story 'The Feeling From Over Here' (featured in *Begin, End, Begin: A #LoveOzYA Anthology*). *Melody Trumpet* is her first children's novel, and she is currently working on another young adult novel and picture book. (Yes, that's why she still hasn't brushed her hair.)

Gabrielle loves sharing her passion for storytelling and creativity with readers and aspiring writers, and has appeared at numerous events including the Sydney Writers' Festival and the Children's Book Council of Australia's national conference.

Say hello: gabrielletozer.com